The Sacred Keys

by

Emma Sumlin

An old map of medieval Ireland is shown. In the center is
the kingdom of Evrydoc, Northwest of it is The Somber
Forest (the page looks charred near there), in the top left
corner is Deeply (the corner is almost fully charred).
Southeast of Evrydoc is Ellison, and in the bottom right
corner is the town of Warwick. In the top right corner is
Summerlin, and in the bottom left corner is Leidleck
Lagoon, and within Leidleck Lagoon it reads Crystallis.

                         ROWAN (V.O.):
               It began with the creation of the
               three keys...

IMAGE: A female elf, glowing white, pours white liquid into
a key mold. She takes the key out and it is glowing.

                         ROWAN (V.O.): (CONT'D)
               The first: The Key of Wisdom. To
               the one it was given to, would
               become very wise, indeed.

IMAGE: A misty blue elf, glowing, pours misty blue liquid
into a key mold. She, also, takes it out and reveals a
shining blue key.

                         ROWAN (V.O.): (CONT'D)
               The second: The Key of Temporary
               Happiness. This key, to whom it
               was given, would grant the one
               present pleasure, but would turn
               into distruction as time passed.

IMAGE: A dark elf, barely glowing, pours black liquid into
a key mold. He takes out the key, and it is a deep black.

                         ROWAN (V.O.): (CONT'D)
               The third key was different. For
               there was no joy found within. It
               was The Key of Corruptness. The
               one who possessed it would become
               greedy and would thirst for
               power...

FADE UP: The camera moves across the map to Leidleck
Lagoon.

                         ROWAN (V.O.): (CONT'D)
               The first key: The Key of Wisdom,
               was given to Rowan Emphedor, the
               mermaid queen.

IMAGE: A beautiful mermaid holds the white key, as if it
were the most valuable thing.

FADE UP: The camera swoops to the center, Evrydoc.

                    ROWAN (V.O.): (CONT'D)
          The second key: The Key of
          Temporary Happiness was given to
          Merlyllson Lassell, the rich king
          of Evrydoc.(pr. Ev-rie-doc)

IMAGE: King Lassell sits in his thrown, mysteriously
grinning as he holds the key.

FADE UP: The camera glides to the charred place of Deeply.

                    ROWAN (V.O.): (CONT'D)
          The final key was given to Lord
          Xerminine (pr. z-erm-in-nine), the
          selfish King of Deeply. His life
          remained ever corrupt.

IMAGE: Lord Xerminine grasps the key greedily, his hands
shaking.

                    ROWAN (V.O.): (CONT'D)
          Beneath each key was a note from
          the Elf who had made it. It stated
          a sacred rule: The Key you hold
          unlocks the Three Doors, but all
          keys must meet in order for them
          to open. Behind the Three Doors
          lies a destiny for the one who
          conquers the quest.

IMAGE: Lord Xerminine, King Lassell, and Rowan Emphedor
read the notes. Lord Xerminine roars in anger; King Lassell
bites his lip, and Rowan Emphedor softly smiles.

                    ROWAN (V.O.): (CONT'D)
          Lord Xerminine was gravely
          angered, for he had no knowing of
          where the other keys ly. So he
          sent whom were known: The Stenes,
          into the world to seek out the
          other two.

IMAGE: Black, ghostly, hooded figures ride off on ghostly
horses into The Somber Forest, and into the foggy night.

                    ROWAN (V.O.): (CONT'D)
          The Stenes were once men
          themselves, but due to the
          corruptness of men, they
          themselves turned to lost souls,
          forever wandering the broken
          world.

IMAGE: The Stenes ride into villages, slaughtering screaming men, women, and children.

>   ROWAN (V.O.): (CONT'D)
>   A warning was sent out into the
>   land, advising King Lassell and
>   Rowan Emphedor to keep their keys
>   safely hidden.

IMAGE: A scroll is handed to King Lassell. He reads and immediatley sends his key away. A messenger hands a worn box to a peasant, which she slips away behind the door quickly.

>   ROWAN (V.O.): (CONT'D)
>   The Key of Temporary Happiness was
>   given to King Lassell's daughter,
>   Ludovica, for safe keeping. She
>   went into hiding as a peasant to
>   avoid question.

IMAGE: Leidleck is swimming with worried mermaids. Rowan hands a land messenger an oyster package. He rides off, stopping in a little village. A rain-beaten sign reads: Warwick.

>   ROWAN (V.O.): (CONT'D)
>   Instead of giving the key to a
>   royal, Rowan gave it to the least
>   of these: a Weewam.

IMAGE: The messenger hands the oyster package to a curly, dark-headed, short, young man. (a.k.a. Edric Grover) He takes it, looking shocked.

<u>FADE TO BLACK</u>

TITLE: **The Sacred Keys**

<u>FADE IN:</u>

EXT. WARWICK -- DAY

Edric Grover is sitting by the sun dappled pond. He skips rocks and hums. From a distance behind him, two Weewams quietly snicker and sneak towards him.

>   MEL:
>   You do it!

>   ADI:
>   No--i did it last time!

                    MEL:
     But i did it last, last time!

                    ADI:
     No i--

                    EDRIC:
     Guys, its about time you figure
     out, i already know you're there.

Edric looks back and grins. Mel looks at Adi.

                    MEL:
     (whispers) You were too loud!

                    ADI:
     (louder) No i wasn't, if you'd
     just excepted my proposal we would
     have--

Edric stands up and walks, putting his hand on their
shoulders.

                    EDRIC:
     Melville Diedrich and Adelheid
     Ogden. The whole village of
     Warwick knows those names. Your
     famous...!

                    ADI:
     Really?

Edric walks on, biting his apple.

                    EDRIC:
     For making trouble.

Adi and Mel continue to argue as Edric walks along the dirt
roads in the finest of moods. He looks at the villagers in
the cotton fields, filling up their wheel barrels with
cotton, corn, tomatoes, and such. From behind an exciting
voice is heard.

                    BARTH:
     Edric!

Edric looks behind at a small wagon. Standing in front in
another short Weewam with curly red hair.

                    EDRIC:
     Barth?

                    BARTH:
     Edric, i can't believe it's you!

Edric walks up to him.

                    EDRIC:
          Barth, you told me you'd be gone
          for two months, it's been three.

                    BARTH:
          What?

They stare at each other. Edric crosses his arms. Suddenley
they both start laughing as Edric's face breaks into a
smile and they leap into each other's arms.

                    EDRIC:
          It's wonderful to see you, Barth!

                    BARTH:
          Wonderful's not the word!

                    EDRIC:
          How've you been?

                    BARTH:
          Great, i can't wait to tell you
          all about my trip when i get the
          chance...Say? Would you might want
          to come and help me unpack?

                    EDRIC:
          My old friend!

Edric puts his hand on Barth's shoulder and they climb into
the wagon.

                                        CUT TO:

EXT. THE FIELDS OF WARWICK.

WIDE ON: The wagon rattles as it passes on the dusty road.

                    EDRIC:
          So tell me, what's Evrydoc like?

                    BARTH:
          Oh, Edric, much more than i
          thought, it was great! The city
          folk much more bustling then ol'
          Warwick.

                                        CLOSE ON:

                    EDRIC:
          Really?

                    BARTH:
          Oh, sure. The town's folk going
          from shop-to-shop--,they have the
          finest bread an' cheese. It's a
          wonder!

                    EDRIC:
          Gee, i wish i could've gone. But i
          had to stay back and tend the
          cotton fields. They're almost in
          bloom.

                    BARTH:
          I love the good smell of cotton.

Barth takes a giant sniff.

                    BARTH: (CONT'D)
          Ah, smells like good ol' Warwick
          again!

Edric laughs.

                                        WIDE ON/CUT TO:

EXT. BAILE (EDRIC'S HOME) -- DAY

The wagon rattles on down the road. Weewams plow the fields
and wave as they pass on by. They pass Weewam homes, some
female Weewams planting mini gardens.

                                        CLOSE ON:

                    BARTH:
          Well i see your home's still in
          shape.

                    EDRIC:
          BAILE (BAL-yeh)is a great place.
          Ah--Barth, would you be so upset
          if i was to grab something inside?

                    BARTH:
          Not at all.

INT. BAILE - DAY

Edric hops out of the wagon and walks into the cottage. It
is dimly lit inside. The floor creaks beneath him as he
walks. He opens the pantry, grabbing bread and cheese.
Suddenley, through a mirror, something catches his
attention: The Key of Wisdom. It is glowing white within

the oyster shell. Out of utter shock, Edric drops the bread
and cheese and rushes to it. He holds it and breathes deep.

                    EDRIC:
          Oh no--

                    BARTH:
          Eh, Edric, you coming?

                    EDRIC:
          Yes, just a minute!

He runs the oyster shell into his messy bedroom and hides
it safely beneath his pillow. He rushes to the kitchen and
picks the bread and cheese up, blows it, and ties it in a
sack.

                                        CUT TO:

EXT. BAILE - DAY

Edric closes Baile's door behind him and heads to the wagon
where Barth is waiting.

                    BARTH:
          What've you got in there, Edric?

                    EDRIC:
          (dazed) Cheese and bread.

                    BARTH:
          Yum.

Edric hops in and they ride off.

                                        CUT TO:

EXT. HAME (BARTH'S HOME) -- EVENING.

Edric and Barth are sitting on the Hame's porch, looking
out at the night sky.

                    BARTH:
          Isn't it just wonderful, the night
          sky?

                    EDRIC:
          Yeah.

                    BARTH:
          I mean, comparing Warwick to
          Evrydoc, it's much calmer. Not a
          care in the world, here, i say. No
          rushing or places to be. Just here
          at the Hame, looking up at the
          stars.

Suddenly a faint sound of cheering, music, and laughter
rises into hearing.

                    BARTH: (CONT'D)
          Blimey, what's going on?

                    EDRIC:
          Oh, it's Finrod's birthday party.

                    BARTH:
          Why aren't we down there? He's
          your own brother an' all!

                    EDRIC:
          Trust me, Barth. He's not
          searching everywhere, wondering
          where we are. He doesn't care.

                    BARTH:
          I care. They're singing and
          dancing, drinkin' ale and cold
          wine!

Edric hesitates.

                    EDRIC:
          Well...alright.

                                        BRIEF CUT TO:

EXT. WARWICK PARTY GROUNDS (THE SQUARE) - NIGHT

Music of bagpipes fill the air. Many Weewams dance, clap,
and sing. Happiness fills the air. Meanwhile Edric and
Barth sit at a wooden table, drinks in front of them. In
the crowd they watch Adi dance with a pretty blonde Weewam.

                    BARTH:
          Lookie there, ol' Adi's dancing
          with Daisy Greendale. I never knew
          him as one to be dancing with
          girls.

                    EDRIC:
          You've missed a lot in three
          months.

They watch Mel ask a red headed girl. She refuses and he
kicks the dirt, walking away. Edric grins.

                    EDRIC: (CONT'D)
          Did you see that?

                    BARTH:
          What?

                    EDRIC:
          Mel asked Emma Broomsteade for a
          dance and she refused him!

Barth isn't paying attention, rather he is watching a brown
headed Weewam serving punch to others.

                    EDRIC: (CONT'D)
          Did you hear me, Barth? Mel asked
          Emma--...Barth?

Edric looks up and sees what Barth is focused on.

                    EDRIC: (CONT'D)
          Well, lookie there.

Edric leans in to Barth's ear.

                    EDRIC: (CONT'D)
          Good ol' Merida Bloom's still
          here, isn't she? Ask her for a
          dance.

                    BARTH:
          Your joking?

                    EDRIC:
          Don't give me that,...ask!

                    BARTH:
          Well, what if she'd refuse me,
          like what happened to Mel?

                    EDRIC:
          That's *normal* for Mel. You, on the
          other hand, are Bartholomew
          Grader, not some troublemaker.

Barth looks like confidence is building up in him. He
straightens his collar.

                    BARTH:
          I'll do it.

                    EDRIC:
          You will?

Barth gets up and walks up to the punch booth. Edric
watches carefully, holding in his laughter. Merida smiles
and he coughs. Edric sees him say something, then Barth
glances at him nervously. Merida smiles and nods. Barth
holds out his hands proudly and she takes it as he sweeps
her to the dance arena. Edric laughs.

                                             CUT TO:

EXT. THE SQUARE - NIGHT

Barth sits down, the dancing has ended. He is blushing
marvelously. Edric smiles as Finrod Grover, Edric's older
brother, stands on a mini stage. He looks exactly like
Edric, but with scruffs.

                    FINROD:
          Weewams and Weewillis's. Thank you
          for attending my thirty second
          birthday party. It is quite an
          honor for you all to celebrate me
          together, i thank you.

Edric rolls his eyes, looking at Barth who chokes a small
laugh.

                    FINROD: (CONT'D)
          As you all must know, i've had
          quite the year. My father Edward,
          and my mother Saige, have passed
          on, bless them. And i have no
          family left.

Edric looks ultimatley confused. He leans over to Barth.

                    EDRIC:
          He's crazy.

Barth nods.

                    FINROD:
          That's why i will begin a new
          journey,...in Ellison.

Weewam's gasp.

                    FINROD: (CONT'D)
          I know this must come as a shock,
          since i've just recentley been
          elected mayor; but not a worry.
          I'd like you to meet our new
          mayor.

Weewams look over the crowd, desparate to get a better view. Edric isn't surprised.

                    FINROD: (CONT'D)
          Meet Christopher Streep.

Weewams clap and a plump Weewam comes on stage.

                    CHRISTOPHER:
          Thank you, everyone. I, ah--

A bloodcurdling scream echoes through the Warwick air. Weewams gasp and look around. Edric seems to know.

                    EDRIC:
          Not now.

The scream fills the air again. Babies cry. Finrod and Christopher look out shocked.

                    CHRISTOPHER:
          Beard of Moses!

Edric immediatley stands.

                    EDRIC:
          Quick! Everyone needs to get to
          safety. It's Lord Xerminine's
          followers--The Stenes!

                    WEEWAM:
          Why have they come?

                    EDRIC:
          They've come for me. They've come
          for the Key of Wisdom.

People shriek. Finrod looks at Edric dead in the eyes with fury.

                    EDRIC: (CONT'D)
          This is not a trick! Go!

Weewams heed his word and scurry off. Finrod fights through the screaming crowd towards Edric. Finrod grabs his arm.

                    FINROD:
          How do you know of the Key of
          Wisdom. Tell me!

Edric fiercly yanks his arm from Finrod's grasp.

                    EDRIC:
          More than you could know. And
          besides, you do have family
          left--it's me, Finrod, Edric
          Grover: your brother!

                    FINROD:
          Half brother!

Edric looks at Barth, feeling frustrated.

                    EDRIC:
          Listen, we have to get the Key out
          of here. That's what Lord
          Xerminine wants.

                    FINROD:
          Why would Warwick possess the Key?

                    EDRIC:
          Because it was entrusted to me.
          The Stenes must have found out
          where it's been hidden these ten
          years.

                    BARTH:
          Ten years? Shows how much you keep
          from your best friend.

                    EDRIC:
          I'm sorry, Barth. Listen, it's at
          the Baile, we have to get it out
          of here. We have to get it back to
          Rowan Emphedor, the Queen of
          Leidleck Lagoon!

Edric runs, Barth, Finrod, and Streep follow. The screams
get louder. Suddenley, as they pass over the bridge, Adi
and Mel run into them.

                    ADI:
          We were worried, Edric!

                    MEL:
          Extremley. We thought the Stenes
          might've gotten to yeh!

                    EDRIC:
          I can't refuse, come on!

All of them run, all the way to the Baile. Edric storms
inside.

                                        CUT TO:

INT. THE BAILE -- MIDNIGHT

Edric races inside, ahead of the others. He runs into the messy bedroom and throws the pillow aside. The Key is glowing brighter than ever before. The others race in.

                    BARTH:
          It's white...the Key of Wisdom!

                    ADI:
          It's glowing bright.

                    MEL:
          Real bright!

                    CHRISTOPHER:
          Why's it glowing, Edric?

                    EDRIC:
          There's only one reason,...The
          Stenes are drawing nearer. We have
          to hide!

                    FINROD:
          But where?

                    EDRIC:
          The cellar,--for ale!

They run out, Edric grabbing a sack and wrapping it around the now, see-through oyster.

                                        CUT TO:

EXT. WARWICK STREETS -- MIDNIGHT

Edric, Barth, Finrod, Adi, Mel, and Christopher race out, Mel lagging behind. They run past cottages and into a small Saloon titled: "The Slimy Slug".

                                        CUT TO:

INT. THE SLIMY SLUG SALOON - MIDNIGHT

Edric, ahead, runs to the back room and slams open a cellar door.

                    EDRIC:
          Quick! Inside!

They all dash inside. Edric slams the cellar door shut.

--Immediate Screen Black

EXT. WARWICK'S ROLLING HILLS - MORNING

The sun rises, beautifully over the rolling hills and
cotton trees.

ANGLE: The Slimy Slug doors.

                                        CUT TO:

INT. THE CELLAR FLOOR - MORNING.

Light beams through the cracks. Edric sleeps peacfully.
Suddenley Barth's

ANGLE: (cont'd) hands tug on Edric and the others to wake
up.

                    BARTH:
          Edric, Mel, Adi! Mr. Finrod, Mr.
          Streep! It's mornin'!

Edric groans as he wakes, squinting in the light.

                    ADI:
          Looks like them Stenes are gone...

                    FINROD:
          This is stupid, hiding in a cellar
          while the whole town went to their
          homes. Edric there's a reason your
          not my brother!

Finrod stands frustrated. Edric ignores him.

                    BARTH:
          What now, Edric?

                    EDRIC:
          I have to leave. It's not long
          before the Stenes come back.

                    MEL:
          Tell us, Edric...the story.

The others prepare to hear. Finrod rolls his eyes.

                    EDRIC:
          Well...ten years ago, it was.

                                        FADE TO:

INT. THE BAILE - NIGHT

IMAGE: It is a peaceful Autumn evening and Edric is eating
a juicy tomato while reading a book on the sofa.

                    EDRIC (V.O.):
          I was having a normal evening in
          the Baile when there was a knock
          on my door.

IMAGE: A rather loud knock is heard.

                    EDRIC:
          Who is it?

There is no answer.

                    EDRIC: (CONT'D)
          Who's there?

Silence. Edric huffs and places his tomato on top of his
book and walks to the door. He opens it. Suddenly a huge
rush of wind blows Edric's curly, dark hair. White light
makes him squint as it floods the room. Suddenley it dies
down and standing there is the messenger, holding open the
oyster, revealing the key and all it's glory.

                    EDRIC (V.O.):
          From the moment i saw it, i knew
          it was the Key of Wisdom. The
          messenger said...

Image: Edric takes the oyster.

                    MESSENGER:
          Queen Rowan Emphedor of Leidleck
          Lagoon, home of the mermaids,
          summons you to be the bearer of
          The Key of Wisdom, as it must be
          hidden.

                    EDRIC:
          Me...why me?

                    MESSENGER:
          It is your destiny. You must hide
          it until the appointed moment,
          then you must help find the
          others, as the prophecy states:
          The Three Keys unlock the Three
          Doors. Within you will find your
          fate--Corruptness, Temporary
          Happiness, or Wisdom. But the
          three must become one.
                    (MORE)

                    MESSENGER: (CONT'D)
          Find them, and unlock The Three
          Doors, within the kingdom of
          Deeply. "If you succeed, wisdom
          you will heed. If you fail,
          destruction must prevail."

                                        CUT TO:

INT. THE CELLAR - MORNING.

                    EDRIC:
          And he left. I knew this would
          happen, and...now i realize, i
          must leave...

                    CHRISTOPHER:
          I see...

                    FINROD:
          (Now intrigued) When must you go,
          Edric?

                    EDRIC:
          Soon,...very soon.

Christopher stands up.

                    CHRISTOPHER:
          You need my permission, Edric. And
          that i grant you with, but only if
          you bring someone with you. Who
          will that be?

                    EDRIC:
          Barth...will you come with me?

                    BARTH:
          What're friends for?

Edric pats him on the shoulder and they smile at each
other.

ANGLE: Mel and Adi look at each other, somewhat
disappointed.

                    CHRISTOPHER:
          Alright,...let's inform Warwick.

Edric nods bravely.

                                        CUT:

EXT. THE SQUARE -- NOON.

Christopher gets on stage and claps to settle the town
down. He signals to Edric and Barth to come up. As they do,
Mel and Adi look dissapointed.

                    CHRISTOPHER:
          Thank you, Weewams and
          Weewillis's, for meeting me here
          this afternoon. After the events
          of last night, there has been some
          explaining. You see,...The Stenes
          were after The Key of Wisdom...

Weewams gasp.

                    CHRISTOPHER: (CONT'D)
          ...Which has been hidden at the
          Baile for nearly ten years. Thanks
          to Edric Grover, the secret has
          been kept. But it's about time for
          the truth to be let in the light.
          Mr. Grover and Bartholomew Grader
          will be taking on the Quest of
          unlocking the Three Doors. It will
          be hard, and it will be
          dangerous...but i couldn't ask for
          braver Weewams then these two
          right here.

Christopher claps, followed by the rest of the Weewams.
Edric and Barth are overcome with emotion.

                    CHRISTOPHER: (CONT'D)
          They will now set off for Deeply,
          in the hopes of meeting a fate of
          Wisdom. So lets give them the
          proper farewell they deserve...

Weewams clap and and Christopher leads them in their
anthem.

                    WEEWAMS:
          In the peaceful land of ours,
          Within the bright green trees,
          There's a kind of love we know,
          That's larger than the bees,
          It's a kind of love that grows,
          In our very hearts right now,
          It's the love of a generation,
          Raining from the clouds,
          Warwick, Warwick,
          From the pond, to the bridge, to
          the seas,
          We hold to this very love,

That's higher than the trees...

All the Weewams clap. Edric smiles at Barth, who is wiping his tears.

                                        CUT TO:

EXT. THE COTTON FIELDS - AFTERNOON

ANGLE: The Weewams wave as Edric and Barth prepare to leave. In the back of the crowd, Mel and Adi scurry to get a better view...

                    EDRIC:
          You ready?

                    BARTH:
          I am, Mr. Grover.

Edric pats him and they step outside of the cotton fields, into the open land. Weewams cheer and wave goodbye.

ANGLE: Mel and Adi in the back.

                    MEL:
          C'mon, let's go.

                    ADI:
          'Righty!

They scurry away from the crowd.

                                        CUT TO:

EXT. OUTSIDE THE COTTON FIELDS - AFTERNOON.

                    EDRIC:
          With that, a very kind farewell,
          we set forth. On a journey that
          will bring us neither right nor
          wrong. A journey that will bring
          peace to all.

                    BARTH:
          Your a good Weewam, Edric.

                    EDRIC:
          To follow me on a dangerous
          journey, Barth, makes you an even
          better one.

Edric and Barth walk out of sight as the crowd cheers on.

<u>**FADE OUT.**</u>

INT. DEEPLY CASTLE -- NIGHT.

The stillness of Deeply Castle is very dark. A deathly faint breathing in heard in the distance. The camera glides upwards revealing Lord Xerminine sits in his throne.

ANGLE: Lord Xerminine's face. - It's a black mask revealing his blue eyes.

Suddenly the Stenes' leader glides in.

                    XERMININE:
          Has it been done as i asked?

A silence is fallen as the Stene leader thinks of what to say.

                    CORPZ:
          (whisper tone) My Lord--

Lord Xerminine slams a rotted wooden staff down and stands in anger.

                    XERMININE:
          I said has it been done?!

                    CORPZ:
          No sir, we couldn't find the
          child.

                    XERMININE:
          Child?...Child? You were looking
          for a child?!

                    CORPZ:
          That's what you described him
          as...

                    XERMININE:
          I described him "childlike" and
          short. You're as stupid as you
          look.

                    CORPZ:
          Forgive me, my Lord.

Corpz bows.

                    XERMININE:
          The one who bears the Key of
          Wisdom is a Weewam.

                    CORPZ:
I understand that, my Lord, but--

                    XERMININE:
But what, Corpz?

                    CORPZ:
We murdered every child in
Summerlin.

                    XERMININE:
Summerlin is filled with "rich"
Weewams. This one lives in
Warwick, the poorest town on the
map!

                    CORPZ:
It will be done, my Lord. That
Weewam must not live another day.

                    XERMININE:
...He is not in Warwick...

                    CORPZ:
By what means?

                    XERMININE:
Summerlin is near enough Warwick,
that he could HEAR YOUR SHRIEKS!

                    CORPZ:
He has gone,...hasn't he?

                    XERMININE:
The Prophecy states a Weewam will
find the Three Keys and unlock the
Three Doors. He has gone to
fulfill it. Let it not be so.

                    CORPZ:
Yesssss, sir.

                                        FADE TO:

EXT. BLAKELY FOREST - SUNSET

Edric and Barth are walking through the small forest.

                    BARTH:
I'm getting real hungry, Edric.

                    EDRIC:
Here...

Edric takes his sack off his shoulder and opens it. He takes out pita bread.

                    BARTH:
          Why thank you.

Edric hands it to him. Barth eats gratefully.

                    BARTH: (CONT'D)
          Don't you want any?

                    EDRIC:
          I can wait till morning. Ellison
          is very close.

                    BARTH:
          But you've hardly eatin' anything
          today?

                    EDRIC:
          That's alright,...i'm not real
          hungry.

Barth shrugs and they keep on walking. Suddenley a rock flies at Barth's head.

                    BARTH:
          Ahh!

Barth falls to thE ground. Edric immediatley turns around looking for anyone around.

                    EDRIC:
          Who's there? I'm not afraid--throw
          a rock at *me*, if you must!

He looks around. Giving up, Edric runs to Barth who's groaning.

                    ADI (V.O.):
          We don't want to throw a rock at
          you, Edric.

Edric looks out.

                    EDRIC:
          Who's there?

Suddenley Adi and Mel come out of the bushes.

                    BARTH:
          Guys?

                    ADI:
          Don't even recognize your fellow
          Weewam's voice, don't you, Edric?

                    EDRIC:
          (furious) Why are you two here?

                    MEL:
          Isn't it obvious? We're coming
          along with you!

Edric stands.

                    EDRIC:
          Don't you realize, it's a
          dangerous quest? Streep only asked
          for me to take Barth. If i needed
          more people, he'd of asked you!

                    MEL:
          Don't take it so harshly, Grover.
          We only want to help you.

                    BARTH:
          I think you've helped, plenty.

                    ADI:
          Sorry about that, Barth. We were
          just trying to make sure it was
          the right Weewams. Didn't want to
          walk right out in the open, with
          the Stenes prowling around.

                    EDRIC:
          Even if you did come along, we
          haven't much food.

                    ADI:
          No worries!

He takes out a stack of sandwiches from his pack. Mel
catches one that nearly falls.

                    MEL:
          We did!

                    BARTH:
          Good Hame, were'd you get all that
          food?

                    ADI:
          Daisy made them.

Mel rolls his eyes.

                    ADI: (CONT'D)
          What's wrong?

                    MEL:
          You an' that Greendale woman,
          again.

                    ADI:
          Just because i asked Daisy for a
          dance, he's angry.

                    BARTH:
          Well, you asked Emma, Mel. You're
          even!

                    MEL:
          Oh, don't you say that! She
          refused!

                    ADI:
          And you good well deserved it,
          Mel.

                    EDRIC:
          Will you two ever learn to get
          along? I mean, how could you ever
          help us return the Key of Wisdom
          to Rowan Emphedor, anyways.

                    MEL:
          Weren't you going to find the
          other two keys, yourself?

                    EDRIC:
          Only Rowan can help us know where
          the others are.

                    ADI:
          'Righty then. How 'bout we head to
          Ellison now. Blakely's creeps are
          going to come out soon.

                    EDRIC:
          Come on, then.

The four begin walking through Blakely forest.

ANGLE: Edric's nervous eyes.

Edric looks down at his closed hands. He opens them and a
bright key shines white light, making the forest glow.
Suddenley the Stenes loud shrieks are heard.

                    EDRIC: (CONT'D)
          Shouldn't have done that--

                    BARTH:
          Edric! The Stenes!

Barth points to the forest behind them. A far distance
away, the Stenes are coming closer.

                    BARTH: (CONT'D)
          Go!

The four terrified, dart as fast as they can through the
forest.

                    MEL:
          How'd they get here so fast!

                    EDRIC:
          It's my fault! The glow of the key
          catches their attention! Hurry!

They run over logs and broken branches. Now the town of
Ellison can be seen.

                    BARTH:
          It's Ellison!

EXT. ELLISON - MIDNIGHT

The four Weewams runs around the corner into an alleyway.
The Stenes' screams make this scene thriller-like.

                    MEL:
          What do we do?

                    EDRIC:
          We need to hide in a light-filled
          place. The Stenes hate the light.

                    BARTH:
          What about at a home?

                    MEL:
          I dunno.

                    ADI:
          Guys...?

                    EDRIC:
          Not a house. But a store might
          work.

                    ADI:
          Guys!

They look at Adi's proud face. His eyes glance up and a
sign reads: The Gentle Giant.

                                        CUT TO:

INT. THE GENTLE GIANT, ELLISON - NIGHT

The four Weewams enter the tavern and they are the shortest
there. Men smoke and drink, staring creepily at them. They
walk up to the counter.

                    BAR TENDER:
          Sorry, only adults aloud.

                    BARTH:
          We are adults, you big loaf!

The bar tender laughs.

                    BAR TENDER:
          Then what are you?

                    EDRIC:
          We are Weewams from the village of
          Warwick!

                    BAR TENDER:
          Children, you mean.

                    BARTH:
          We're not--!

                    EDRIC:
          Don't fight it, Barth.

Barth looks fumed.

                    BAR TENDER:
          Then how old *are* you all?

                    EDRIC:
          Over 21.

                    BAR TENDER:
          ...I'll take your word for it.
          C'mon, i'll get you seated.

Edric looks at them in relief and they follow him into the
back corner.

                    BAR TENDER: (CONT'D)
          What would you like?

                    MEL:
          Four ales--

                    ADI:
          --Five ales, thank you.

                    MEL:
          Five?

Adi smiles stupidly.

                    BAR TENDER:
          Alright.

He walks off mumbling.

                    BAR TENDER: (CONT'D)
          Kids these days...

                                        CUT TO:

EXT. OUTSIDE THE TAVERN - NIGHT

Rain starts to pour and The Stenes search Ellison. The only
lit building is The Gentle Giant.

                    CORPZ:
          They're in the tavern...We'll feed
          before dawn...

They glide off.

                                        CUT TO:

INT. THE GENTLE GIANT - MIDNIGHT

Tiredly Barth, Mel, and Adi slump in bed. Edric is at the
window.

                    BARTH:
          Come to bed, Edric. It's been a
          long day.

                    EDRIC:
          Not with the Stenes on the loose.
          The Gentle Giant is the only place
          open all night in Ellison. No
          doubt, the Stenes know we're here.

                    BARTH:
          How about we take the night shift,
          Edric?

                    MEL:
          That's a good idea.

Adi nods.

                    EDRIC:
          Alright. I'll wake Barth up in
          three hours, he'll watch an hour.
          Then Barth, you can wake Mel and
          Adi up for the last two.

                    ADI:
          Why both of us?

                    EDRIC:
          In your case, two is better than
          one.

                                        CUT TO:

INT. THE GENTLE GIANT - 4AM

It has been four hours and Barth wakes both Mel and Adi up.
They groan but still get up.

                    BARTH:
          Wake up. You've got two hours!

Barth gets in bed.

                                        CUT TO:

INT. THE GENTLE GIANT - BARELY DAWN

Corpz and other Stenes glide into the room. Barth's eyes
immediatley sense something is wrong.

ANGLE: Adi and Mel have fallen asleep.

Edric is still peacefully sleeping. Barth slowly opens the
bedside drawer when the Stenes aren't looking. He takes out
a blade. Suddenly he tries to stab one.

                    BARTH:
          Ahh!

The rest wake. Corpz laughs.

                    CORPZ:
          You think you could outsmart us,
          Weewam man.

Barth shrinks back, holding the blade.

> CORPZ: (CONT'D)
> Give us the Key of Wisdom, and you
> may go free...refuse, and you will
> all die.

Mel looks at Edric worridly. Corpz notices.

> CORPZ: (CONT'D)
> I see. The dark headed Weewam
> carries it.

He glides over and flings the covers off Edric.

> CORPZ: (CONT'D)
> Don't you!

> EDRIC:
> No, sir.

> CORPZ:
> You dare lie to me, Weewam!

> EDRIC:
> I'm not lying.

> CORPZ:
> Slit his throat!

A Stene grabs the blade from Barth's hand and grabs Edric, holding the blade to his neck.

> BARTH:
> No!

The Stenes all look at Barth. Edric signals to Barth not to tell.

> BARTH: (CONT'D)
> Uh--we hid it underneath the soil,
> b-back in Blakely!

> CORPZ:
> Did you?

Corpz comes close to Barth's face. Barth gulps.

> CORPZ: (CONT'D)
> Did you...

> BARTH:
> Don't hurt him, please!

> CORPZ:
> They lie.

Stenes circle closer. Barth winces nervously.

                    CORPZ: (CONT'D)
          Tell us...the truth.

                    BARTH:
          Uh--

The Stene holds the knife closer to Edric's neck.

                    BARTH: (CONT'D)
          It's--

Suddenley the door slams open. A handsome, brave warrior
rushes in.

                    SIR LAURENCE:
          Unhand him, you foul beast!

Corpz looks back at Sir Laurence and some Stenes fling for
him. Instead of flashing his sword at them he, and some
other men shine lanterns at them. The Stenes shriek very
loud. The Stene drops Edric and he holds his neck. The
Stenes flee out the open window. Silence. Edric coughs.

                    EDRIC:
          Who are you?

A cheerful grin crosses the young knight's face. He holds
out his hand and Edric and the others awkwardly shake it.

                    SIR LAURENCE:
          Sir Laurence of Swanzy.

                    MEL:
          Swanzy? I've never heard of such a
          place.

                    SIR LAURENCE:
          It is a small kingdom, but an
          honorable one!

Edric stands up in utter shock of the previous events.

                    EDRIC:
          T-thank you, Sir. You saved us.

                    SIR LAURENCE:
          (Smiling) My pleasure, lad. But
          might i ask why you were being
          hunted by Stenes?

                    ADI:
          He has the Key of Wisdom, Sir.

Sir Laurence's smile drops to seriousness. He walks closer.

>   SIR LAURENCE:
>   *The* Key of Wisdom?

Barth nods.

>   SIR LAURENCE: (CONT'D)
>   ...I believed it was just a tale.

>   EDRIC:
>   No, Sir...It's true. We've been
>   sent to find Rowan Emphedor, the
>   mermaid queen. I believe she can
>   help us locate the other two.

>   SIR LAURENCE:
>   Ah, the other two. The Key of
>   Temporary Happiness and The Key of
>   Corruptness, i believe. My mother
>   believed so much in them. I was
>   foolish enough not to care. But
>   now things have changed,...since
>   her death.

Edric walks closer to Sir Laurence.

>   EDRIC:
>   Would you, perhaps, like to come
>   along with us? We could use a
>   brave knight like you.

>   SIR LAURENCE:
>   Positively!

>   ADI:
>   We're only Weewams.

Sir Laurence bends down to Adi.

>   SIR LAURENCE:
>   Weewams, my lad, are one of the
>   bravest creatures i know.

Adi smiles faintly. Sir Laurence stands with a bright
smile.

>   SIR LAURENCE: (CONT'D)
>   Alright, shall we be off?

>   EDRIC:
>   Yes, but, what if the Stenes come
>   back?

                    SIR LAURENCE:
          They will try. But with four
          Weewams, a knight, and a bright
          lantern, they don't stand a
          chance.

Sir Laurence straightens his back and walks on out. Edric,
Barth, Mel, and Adi smile at each other like a load of
courage was placed upon them.

                                        CUT TO:

EXT. THE STABLES, ELLISON - SUNRISE.

Sir Laurence leads them down a dirt road into horse
stables. The four Weewams scurry behind him.

                    BARTH:
          Ugh! Smells like when Mrs. Palmer
          dumps the sewage!

                    SIR LAURENCE:
          Horse dung!

Barth and the others notice Sir Laurence untying a couple
of horses at a time.

                    EDRIC:
          Why do we need horses?

Sir Laurence smiles.

                    SIR LAURENCE:
          You don't expect a knight to walk
          the way to Leidleck Lagoon, do
          you?

Sir Laurence leads a horse to Edric who looks dumbstruck.

                    SIR LAURENCE: (CONT'D)
          Here you are, Weewam.

                    EDRIC:
          I'm Edric Grover, Sir.

                    SIR LAURENCE:
          Forgive me for not questioning
          your names.

                    MEL:
          Not a problem! I'm Mel and this is
          my best friend Adi.

Sir Laurence nods in approval.

                    BARTH:
          Barth Grader, Sir. Are you sure we
          could fit on them horses? They
          look mighty big.

                    SIR LAURENCE:
          Of course. One thing that i find
          very generous is the stables
          contain...

He takes down a wooden stool from the wall.

                    SIR LAURENCE: (CONT'D)
          ...A step!

Edric looks nervously at Barth.

                                        CUT TO:

EXT. ELLISON STREETS - DAY

Five horses gallop out the exit of Ellison into the great
green land, surrounded by mountains and breathtaking
waterfalls.

                                        CUT TO:

                                        FADE UP:

EXT. ASHVALE VALLEY LANDS - DAY.

The horses come to a stop and all five of them are in a
row: Sir Laurence, Mel, Adi, Edric, and Barth. They stare
at the beauty of Ashvale.

                    MEL:
          Wawick is nice, but when you see
          other parts of Ashvale, it sure
          takes your breath away.

                    SIR LAURENCE:
          And it's only just begun. Leidleck
          Lagoon and Evrydoc are the last
          bit of beautiful Ashvale has to
          offer. Once you reach The Somber
          Forest...

The rest admire the beauty but Edric. He secretley looks
down at the Key, somewhat burdened by it.

                                        CUT:

INT. THE TORTURE CHAMBERS OF DEEPLY - DAY

The deep black clouds do not reveal a single tread of light
in Deeply. Lord Xerminine walks the torture chambers,
waiting mysteriously. Suddenley the doors burst open and a
woman is brought in. Her hair is messy red and she is very
freckled. The Stenes drag her along as she cries.

                    XERMININE:
          I thank you for coming.

She is thrown at the ground at his feet, silently weeping.

                    XERMININE: (CONT'D)
          Why do you cry?

                    BLUEMIST:
          You've taken everything!

                    XERMININE:
          Not everything...

He tilts her tear stained face towards his mask, blue eyes
shining.

                    XERMININE: (CONT'D)
          You still have your life.

                    BLUEMIST:
          You killed my brother,...you
          killed my family...

                    XERMININE:
          Yes, i did. But now, you will work
          for me.

                    BLUEMIST:
          Never. I will never work for you!

                    XERMININE:
          Then you will suffer as all your
          people did!

Bluemist begins to sob aloud.

                    XERMININE: (CONT'D)
          Bring her!

He walks to a table. The Stenes drag her and throw her
against it.

                    XERMININE: (CONT'D)
          You know what to do.

                    STENE:
         Yes, my Lord.

Lord Xerminine walks off down a corridor. The Stenes strip
her as she continuously weeps. Only her shoulders and back
can be seen. They lay her on the table violently, her head
bangs hard on it. A Stene holds a needle, connected to a
wooden box and drags it close to her arm. She watches the
needle, tears pouring down her cheeks. Once it touches her
skin she screams. He pulls it away.

                    STENE: (CONT'D)
         Feel anything?

                    BLUEMIST:
         Please (sobs), please let me free!

Furiously the Stene sticks the needle into her arm. She
screams louder than anything ever heard. Then the Stene
sticks a few more into her legs and shoulders. Screams
rattle the room.

ANGLE: A far distance away we see her shaking from the pain
and the Stene walks out of sight, leaving her alone.

                                             CUT:

EXT. LEIDLECK LAGOON - SUNSET.

Edric hops off his horse.

ANGLE: His face stares in awe at the beautiful lagoon.

The rest hop off their horses looking around. The place is
quiet except for a mermaid woman plucking a harp as she
sits on a rock.

                    ADI:
         Mighty, she's beautiful.

                    BARTH:
         This place is beautiful.

Sir Laurence walks next to them.

                    SIR LAURENCE:
         Indeed. We have now reached
         Leidleck Lagoon.

They walk up to the mermaid.

                    MERMAID:
         You must be looking for Rowan
         Emphedor?

                    EDRIC:
     Yes, mam.

                    MERMAID:
     You will need these...

She hands them each a sack made from a bubble.

                    MEL:
     What is it?

                    MERMAID:
     Swallow it, and you may breathe in
     our world.

All five of them slip it into their mouths.

                    MERMAID: (CONT'D)
     Come along with me.

She puts her harp aside and dives in. The five dive after
her.

                                        CUT TO:

INT. CRYSTALLIS - NIGHT.

Underwater is lit by the bubble houses glowing with
lanterns. The sight of the kingdom is breathtaking.

                    MERMAID:
     Welcome to Crystallis.

As they swim deeper mermaids and mermen swim past. Mel and
Adi seem in Heaven every time they see a lady. Finally they
reach the castle gates.

                    MERMAID: (CONT'D)
     Here i leave you. Rowan Emphedor
     is inside.

                    SIR LAURENCE:
     Thank you, Ms.

She nods and swims off. Suddenley the shell doors open and
a glorious amount of light floods the waters. When the
light dissovles two knight mermen bow to them.

                    ROWAN (V.O.):
     You may enter, servants of good.

The five swim in and light clears away and Rowan, a dark
skinned, dark haired, blue eyed mermaid is staring into

their eyes. You can tell in their eyes she is the most
beautiful woman they've ever seen. The five bow.

                    SIR LAURENCE:
          My Queen.

Rowan grins.

                    ROWAN:
          Welcome, brave warriors of
          Ashvale. You must be very thirsty
          from your journey this far. Please
          (more)

A merman swims over, holding a tray of glasses.

                    ROWAN: (CONT'D)
          (cont'd) have a drink.

They each take a glass. She watches them carefully.
Suddenly Sir Laurence coughs.

Rowan's eyes look towards him.

                    SIR LAURENCE:
          Forgive me, your highness. I am
          Sir Laurence of Swanzy.

He bows. She grins, satisfied.

                    BARTH:
          Bartholomew Grader, Ms.

Barth bows, embarrased.

                    MEL:
          Melville Diedrich, Madam.

Mel bows.

                    ADI:
          Adelheid Ogden, my lady.

Adi bows, slipping a wink. This makes Rowan smile. Her eyes
glide to Edric, who mysteriously looks about to cry.

                    EDRIC:
          E-Edric Grover.

He bows. Rowan rises.

                    ROWAN:
          What you have drank is a magical
          mist.
                    (MORE)

                    ROWAN: (CONT'D)
          It forces one to confess their
          true identity. Now i know, you are
          the ones.

Rowan smiles.

                    ROWAN: (CONT'D)
          I believe i entrusted the Key of
          Wisdom to one of you...

She turns her eyes to Edric, who's eyes are flooded.

                    ROWAN: (CONT'D)
          Mr. Grover...

Edric takes the oyster shell out from his pocket and hands
it to Rowan. She carefully opens it. The white Key is not
glowing but still looks beautiful.

                    ROWAN: (CONT'D)
          Mr. Grover...may i speak to you,
          privately?

Edric looks at Barth and Barth signals him to go on. Edric
nervously nods and swims after her and out the door of the
castle.

INT. THE WATER - NIGHT

As they swim past the bubble house, mermaids and mermen bow
to her. Children cut in to see. Finally they reach the top.

                                             CUT TO:

EXT. LEIDLECK LAGOON - NIGHT.

Edric climbs out and sits on the grass. As Rowan gets out,
her tail fades into a shimmery, silky, skirt. The moon
makes Leidleck Lagoon beautiful. She sits next to him.

                    ROWAN:
          Speak to me...

                    EDRIC:
          I-i don't know what to say.

Rowan lifts his face with her hand.

                    ROWAN:
          Edric,...i see in your eyes: fear.

Edric looks down at the water.

                    ROWAN: (CONT'D)
          I'm afraid too.

Edric looks up, avoiding her eyes.

                    ROWAN: (CONT'D)
          If it were up to me i'd never
          wanted the Key. Overtime it
          becomes a burden.

                    EDRIC:
          I figured.

                    ROWAN:
          Tell me your heart.

                    EDRIC:
          I'm overwhelmed. I wish the Key
          had never been given to me. I'm
          too weak.

                    ROWAN:
          Your not weak, Edric. Your strong.
          But only will you feel strong when
          you believe you are.

                    EDRIC:
          That's not it...It's my
          brother--well, not my brother.

                    ROWAN:
          I don't understand.

                    EDRIC:
          Oh, it's nothing--it doesn't
          matter.

                    ROWAN:
          As you wish.

Edric stands up. Rowan stands, obviously taller.

                    ROWAN: (CONT'D)
          Listen to me, Edric. You have been
          chosen. It might seem difficult
          now, but i am confident your
          destiny will ly with wisdom.
          You've been given
          Wisdom,...remember that...

Edric stands there deep in thought.

                                              CUT:

INT. TORTURE CHAMBERS, DEEPLY - MORNING

The gloominess of Deeply castle is sickening. Bluemist lies on the table, now dressed in black scraps. She looks neither dead nor alive.

ANGLE: Her face lying still starts to shake.

She wakes. A silent tear rolls down her cheek. She looks to the side. Frightfully, Corpz is sitting next to her. He smiles wickedly.

                    CORPZ:
          Comfortable?

She doesn't answer. He leans in somewhat disgusted.

                    CORPZ: (CONT'D)
          Tell me your name, girl!

                    BLUEMIST:
          I won't.

Corpz stands and glides across the room to the Stretcher.

                    CORPZ:
          We have other alternatives. And if
          you'd like to avoid them, i
          suggest you speak!

A silence is followed. Fury fills Bluemist's eyes.

                    BLUEMIST:
          My name is Rose. Rose Edwina.

                    CORPZ:
          Is it?

                    BLUEMIST:
          Yes.

Corpz takes out a knife from his coat and begins to sharpen it.

                    CORPZ:
          Every lie will cost you a part.
          Which one first...how about: your
          wrist!

                    BLUEMIST:
          It's Bluemist! (sobs) Bluemist!
          Now, let me free!

                    CORPZ:
          Of course,...get up!

She lays still on the table.

                    CORPZ: (CONT'D)
               (sarcastically) You--you
          don't want to be free?

                    BLUEMIST:
          I can't move!

Corpz slams down his knife on a chair and glides over to
the table. He grabs her arm and throws her off. She screams
and looks up at him.

                    BLUEMIST: (CONT'D)
          Now i see the truth,...i'm not
          really free.

                    CORPZ:
          No, no your not. You will rot in
          the dungeon, unless someone come
          save you. No one will come for
          such filth.

He grabs her wrist and drags her to the dungeon door. He
stands her up and opens the door. Inside there is stairs
leading to the cold bottom. Bluemist looks at him, eyes
watered, and weakly walks down the steps. Corpz slams the
door.

                                        BLACK SCREEN:

EXT. LEIDLECK LAGOON - NOON

Sir Laurence, Mel, Adi, Barth, and Edric are standing in a
row towards the lagoon water. Rowan is standing near them.

                    ROWAN:
          Now,...it is time.

                    ADI:
          Y-you mean your not coming along?

                    ROWAN:
          Why, no.

                    MEL:
          Then, by gosh, why'd we come here?

                    ROWAN:
          So i can give you this...

She hands Edric a map of Deeply. The grounds and such.

                    MEL:
          It's a blueprint?

                    EDRIC:
          It's a map. A map of Deeply.

                    ROWAN:
          Most every entrance and exit is
          guarded by Stenes. This map will
          glow the entrances, when you
          arrive, that aren't guarded.

                    MEL:
          But you said all were guarded?

                    ROWAN:
          I said most. Now...

A deep depression rolls over Rowan.

                    SIR LAURENCE:
          My queen?

                    ROWAN:
          Someone's in grave
          danger...someone you love,
          Laurence.

Confusion rolls over him.

                    SIR LAURENCE:
          There isn't anyone but you, Madam.
          My--the rest of my loved ones were
          murdered in Summerlin...

                    BARTH:
          The night the Stenes came?

Sir Laurence doesn't answer. The rest look worridley at
each other.

                    ROWAN:
          No...not all of them.

She falls into a merman's arms.

                    MERMAN:
          She's ill.

                    ROWAN:
          Go!

Nervously the others board their horses and ride off.

                                             CUT TO:

EXT. ASHVALE MOUNTAINS - AFTERNOON.

Their horses ride across the land. Over hills, and through forests, past creeks, as the sun sets.

                                        CUT TO:

EXT. BLAKELY - NIGHT.

A fire crackles as Sir Laurence starts it. Edric hops off his horse and kneels down next to Sir Laurence as he picks the fire.

                    EDRIC:
          What happened the night of the
          Stenes?

                    SIR LAURENCE:
          Tt isn't worth mentioning.

Edric looks down not knowing what to say. In the background Mel and Adi are arguing.

                    SIR LAURENCE: (CONT'D)
          We were visiting Summerlin...

Edric looks up.

                    SIR LAURENCE: (CONT'D)
          We heard the shrieks of the
          Stenes. Before we knew it they
          were pouring in the town. My
          father was struck in the head--my
          mother, s-she was impaled...

He winces at the thought. Edric looks very serious.

                    SIR LAURENCE: (CONT'D)
          My sister was--was taken...

A tear rolls down his face.

                    SIR LAURENCE: (CONT'D)
          I doubt she's remained alive...

Edric places his hand on Sir Laurence's shoulder.

                    EDRIC:
          We must have hope....Hope is
          what's gotten us this far, isn't
          it?

Edric pats him and walks towards his pallet. He lays down. Barth is sleeping next to him. Edric smiles faintly and glances back where Sir Laurence is still sitting. Edric closes his eyes, preparing to sleep.

                                        CUT:

EXT. BLAKELY FOREST - MORNING.

The birds chirp as Barth wakes Edric.

                    BARTH:
          Edric. I'm sorry but it's time to
          wake. We're going over to
          Finrod's.

Edric slowly sits up.

                    EDRIC:
          He's moved already?

                    BARTH:
          Oh, yes. Left along time ago, he
          did. And Sir Laurence brought back
          some news while you were asleep...

                    EDRIC:
          What news?

                    BARTH:
          Finrod's got himself a girlfriend.

Barth stands and throws a bucket of water on the fire. Edric stands up, rather shocked.

                    EDRIC:
          A girlfriend? Your joking.

Barth shakes his head.

                    BARTH:
          Nope, not.

Edric smiles.

                    EDRIC:
          What's her name?

                    BARTH:
          Don't know yet.

Edric looks around at the empty camp.

                    EDRIC:
          Where's the others?

                    BARTH:
          Blimey, Edric! They've gone to
          Finrod's already. Wanted to let
          you sleep.

Edric looks at the horses.

                    EDRIC:
          We'd better be going. I'm sure the
          horses would like a stretch.

                                        CUT TO:

INT. FINROD'S HOME "GROVE", ELLISON - DAY

Inside is bustling. Sir Laurence, Barth, Mel, Adi, Edric,
Finrod, and his girlfriend Lucee Lee sit around a table.

                    BARTH:
          So tell us her name, Finrod?

Finrod pats Lucy's shoulders and smiles. She blushes.

                    FINROD:
          This is Lucee Lee, everyone. She's
          a beauty, isn't she?

                    SIR LAURENCE:
          Most certainly.

Finrod looks at Edric who isn't paying attention.

                    FINROD:
          Well, Edric?

Edric looks at her and barely smiles.

                    EDRIC:
          Charming.

Finrod's smile drops. He then turns the phrase around.

                    FINROD:
          Uh--indeed she is. Most charming
          Weewam i ever saw.

                    LUCEE:
          Oh, Finrod, you musn't.

Barth looks at Edric concerned.

                    FINROD:
          Yes, indeed. We met at The Gentle
          Giant. Quite the place, it is. She
          was a waitress.

                    LUCEE:
          He asked for a water! Can't you
          believe it? Just water! That
          surprised me and i loved him for
          being so mature.

Edric rolls his eyes.

                    FINROD:
          I told her a week later i'd loved
          her and she admitted--

                    LUCEE:
          I admitted i did too!

                    FINROD:
          I've now decided someday, for her
          to fill the hole of family inside
          me--

Edric slams his hands on the table furiously.

                    EDRIC:
          I am your brother!

All look at him. Lucee seems shocked.

                    EDRIC: (CONT'D)
          You seem to neglect that, don't
          you, Finrod? You seem to forget
          that our father was one man. A
          great one, i might add. And you
          don't need some spoiled young lady
          to fill that hole, you have me!
          Me!

Edric storms out. Barth wipes his mouth and gets up,
following him.

                    MEL:
          That isn't Edric, really Ms.
          Lucee.

                                             CUT TO:

EXT. OUTSIDE OF "GROVE" - AFTERNOON.

Edric sits on the porch furious. Barth walks and stands
behind him.

                    BARTH:
          What's bothering you, Mr. Edric?

                    EDRIC:
          He's selfish, that Finrod. Doesn't
          care about anyone. Bet he doesn't
          even care about Lucee.

Barth sits by him.

                    BARTH:
          That's not the issue, Edric.
          Finrod was very gracious to invite
          you. He's changed some, Edric.
          It's you...your jealous.

                    EDRIC:
          Jealous? Have you lost it, Barth?

                    BARTH:
          I don't think he meant what he
          said. Before you came inside he
          was chattering all about you.

Edric stays silent.

                    BARTH: (CONT'D)
          He talked about your bravery. Mr.
          Edric, i think you should give 'em
          a chance.

                    EDRIC:
          He didn't give me a chance.

                    BARTH:
          C'mon. Let's get inside. Ms. Lucee
          Lee is bringing out some pudding.

                    EDRIC:
          No, Barth. I will stay.

Barth stays silent and walks inside.

                                                  CUT:

EXT. ELLISON GATES - MORNING.

Sir Laurence and they rest of the Weewams sit on their
horses near the exit gate of Ellison.

                    ADI:
          Where're we off to today, Sir?

SIR LAURENCE:
If i know the map right, we are
nearest to the kingdom of Evrydoc.
If i heard correctly, the Key of
Temporary Happiness lies there.
Pray the king will have enough
faith to give it up.

MEL:
He knows the prophecy, doesn't he?

SIR LAURENCE:
One thing to know about King
Lassell. He's only interested in
one thing: Temporary Happiness and
things of the earth, that are not
eternal.

They ride off.

BARTH:
Edric, has Rowan returned the Key?

EDRIC:
Yes, Barth. She has.

ADI:
Poor Ms. I wonder if she's any
well.

SIR LAURENCE:
One thing i know. She's a warrior.
She'll fight.

CUT TO:

INT. DEEPLY DUNGEON - MORNING.

Barely any light shines through the cell window. Bluemist
is seated against the stone wall. She looks around weakly.
Skeleton's and rotting bodies lay on the floor. Her eyes
water to the brim and she looks at the window.

BLUEMIST:
(praying) Will you not help me. I
have been rid of everything i
love. All my hopes and dreams have
gone. I am left till death. Will
you not send hope?

She fades to unconciousness.

FADE TO CUT:

EXT. EVRYDOC GATES - DAY.

The horses arrive as the guards come forth.

                    GUARD:
          State your form of business in the
          kingdom of Evrydoc.

                    SIR LAURENCE:
          We are The Solidarity to a sacred
          treasure. We have promised to keep
          it safe. We must speak to the
          King.

                    GUARD:
          We shan't make promises. Please
          proceed.

He opens the gates and their horses ride through.

EXT. EVRYDOC VILLAGE - DAY

ANGLE: The outer village. Peasants and such roam around the
city. A dark headed (Ludovica) begs on the side.

                    LUDOVICA:
          Please rich men. Do you not care
          for the poor?

Barth tosses her a coin.

                    LUDOVICA: (CONT'D)
          Thank you for your kindness...

As they enter more people whisper.

                    WOMAN:
          It's a knight! He has come to
          deliver us!

Sir Laurence turns to Edric.

                    SIR LAURENCE:
          We're quite popular.

                    EDRIC:
          Anybody with horses are.

                    SIR LAURENCE:
          Pardon me, Edric, but is something
          the matter?

                    EDRIC:
          No sir. I'm perfectly normal.

Edric rides ahead as Sir Laurence disagrees.

                                        BRIEF CUT TO:

EXT. OUTSIDE OF THE CASTLE - DAY.

They reach the gates. This part is more silenced and calm.

                    MEL:
          Aren't there any guards?

It is obvious there is no one outside.

                    SIR LAURENCE:
          Yes, Melville. Plenty, you just
          wait.

Sir Laurence leads their horses to the gate. As they draw
nearer a loud noise is heard a the gates open. From inside
there, on either sides, are a long row of guards.

                    MEL:
          Blimey.

They ride their horses through the courtyard. As they draw
nearer they get off and tie them to the willow trees.

                    BARTH:
          Isn't it wonderful, Mr. Edric?

                    EDRIC:
          I find Warwick more.

Barth looks annoyed and concerned at Edric's negative
behavior. The five ride to the royal stables, which is East
of the entrance gates. Climbing off they look around.

                    ADI:
          Evrydoc is more green than
          Warwick's cotton fields in the
          springtime.

                    SIR LAURENCE:
          Shall we permit forth?

From a distance many guards walk towards them.

                    BARTH:
          Goodness, Mr. Edric!

                    EDRIC:
          It's the King.

The guards near them, splitting in two rows, allowing King
Lassell to pass through. The five kneel down.

                    MERLYLLSON:
          Welcome, foreigners to Evrydoc.

                    SIR LAURENCE:
          Thank you, your highness.

                    MERLYLLSON:
          Why, you must be thirsty? Get them
          something to drink. Come, come,
          it's getting hot.

                                             CUT TO:

INT. EVRYDOC CASTLE - AFTERNOON

The five follow King Lassell into the palace entrance.
Inside is glittering with gold statues and stone.

                    MERLYLLSON:
          Please, look around. You will find
          possessions from Rome, England,
          and even France. I take pride in
          my home.

                    MEL:
          It's very fine, Sir.

                    ADI:
          I'd say.

They walk into a dining room with a long, silver table. A
banquet is already prepared.

                    MERLYLLSON:
          Please, eat. Be satisfied!

They sit down in huge chairs, dwarfing the Weewams.
Servants bring in wine. Given a glass, Adi smiles greedily.

                    MERLYLLSON: (CONT'D)
          Now tell me, why have you come?

Sir Laurence glances at Edric.

                    MERLYLLSON: (CONT'D)
          I see the dark headed Weewam will
          tell me?

Edric sits up best he can.

                    EDRIC:
          I have been named bearer of the
          Key of Wisdom--

King Lassell puts down his cup, interested.

                    EDRIC: (CONT'D)
          --precisley ten years ago. The
          Great Prophecy states i am to
          bring all three keys to unlock the
          Three Doors. We've come to ask--

King Lassell breaks into laughter.

                    MERLYLLSON:
          Are you expecting me to just hand
          over my Key?

                    BARTH:
          Your highness--

                    MERLYLLSON:
          (Angered) Not a chance.

Sir Laurence stands.

                    SIR LAURENCE:
          King Lassell, it has been
          prophecied for ages. You have no
          choice!

                    MERLYLLSON:
          And what if i don't?

                    SIR LAURENCE:
          With all do respect, we would get
          it somehow.

                    MERLYLLSON:
          You couldn't, even if you tried. I
          have sent it away. Somewhere,
          beyond the rich residences of
          Evrydoc.

                    SIR LAURENCE:
          We will have it by the end of the
          night, my lord.

                    MERLYLLSON:
          I will not lock you up, even
          though you deserve it greatly for
          you arrogance. I am the one who is
          high, don't you forget that.
                    (MORE)

                    MERLYLLSON: (CONT'D)
          But trust me when i say this: You
          will not find it.

King Lassell storms out, guards following behind him.

                                              CUT:

INT. DEEPLY DUNGEON - NIGHT

Bluemist looks dead on the cold floor. Her face in filthy
and blue/grey. Moonlight shines through the barred window.

ANGLE: Bluemist's "dead" body.

A shadow casts, dimming the dungeon even further. A small
person removes a bar and slips through. His body is not yet
shown. As he nears closer, Bluemist wakes started.

                    BLUEMIST:
          Get away!

She backs up to the wall. The man takes off his hood,
revealing his face. He has messy brown hair and a short
beard.

                    GWYDION:
          No need to be alarmed, Ms. I have
          come to save you...

                    BLUEMIST:
          Save me?

                    GWYDION:
          Yes.

Bluemist takes a good look at him.

                    BLUEMIST:
          If you don't mind me asking...what
          are you?

                    GWYDION:
          Mighty, Ms.! You've never seen a
          dwarf before?

                    BLUEMIST:
          Sorry, not in a long while.

                    GWYDION:
          Never mind. We have to get.

> BLUEMIST:
> (Chuckles) I'm in no condition to
> walk.

> GWYDION:
> Shan't you worry, Ms. We'll have
> you out in a bit! Now, first
> things first.

Gwydion takes a clean dress from his satchel.

> GWYDION: (CONT'D)
> You might want something fresh to
> wear?

Astonished, Bluemist takes the dress.

> BLUEMIST:
> How can i ever thank you?

> GWYDION:
> By changing into it. But before
> you do: might you have the energy
> to hoist me up so i can gather the
> ropes?

> BLUEMIST:
> I'll try.

She lifts him with every ounce of strength. Gwydion then
climbs through the bars and out into the Deeply courtyard.

EXT. DEEPLY COURTYARD - MIDNIGHT.

Gwydion pulls a rope out of the horse's carrier, attatched
to its side. He then climbs back into the window.

> CUT TO:

INT. DEEPLY DUNGEON - MIDNIGHT.

Just as Gwydion hops to the floor, Bluemist puts on the
top.

> GWYDION:
> Now, together, we'll throw the
> ropes up and around a window bar.

> BLUEMIST:
> Alright.

> GWYDION:
> One, two, three!

They throw the rope securely around a bar.

                    GWYDION: (CONT'D)
          I'll go first, then i'll hoist you
          up.

Gwydion climbs up the rope. Bluemist watches him.

                    BLUEMIST:
          (Mumbles) Thank you.

Gwydion, now at the top, reaches his hand.

                    GWYDION:
          Grab my hand!

Bluemist reaches and grabs. He pulls her up. Looking into
his eyes, crying she says:

                    BLUEMIST:
          Thank you so much.

Gwydion smiles.

                                             CUT:

EXT. EVRYDOC CASTLE- NIGHT.

The five hide on the side of the castle.

                    ADI:
          What're we to do?

                    SIR LAURENCE:
          We shall not enter the castle.

                    BARTH:
          Shouldn't it be inside, Sir?

                    SIR LAURENCE:
          One thing you've got to know about
          King Lassel is, he's smart. Not as
          smart as her highness but smart
          enough as himself. Don't you
          remember his little saying?

                    MEL:
          Little saying?

Sir Laurence grins.

                    EDRIC:
          "You couldn't, even if you tried.
          I have sent it away."

                    SIR LAURENCE:
          Exactly, Edric! He has sent it
          away. But he'd of had to send it
          to someone he trusts, someone he's
          known some time!

                    BARTH:
          What're you getting at, Sir
          Laurence?

Sir Laurence smiles.

                    SIR LAURENCE:
          Ludovica Lassell.

                    MEL:
          Is it the Princess?

                    SIR LAURENCE:
          Indeed!

                    ADI:
          Do you think she's married?

                    MEL:
          Oh, Adi!

                    BARTH:
          But wouldn't she reside within?

                    SIR LAURENCE:
          Anyone with the key is surely
          suspected royal. But as i said,
          Lassell's a smart pip. The
          Princess is disguised--as a
          commoner, most likely the lowest
          of low.

                    EDRIC:
          A peasant.

                    ADI:
          Wow, my brave knight. You're one
          stallion to come up with that ol'
          brain work.

Sir Laurence begins to walk, grinning.

                    SIR LAURENCE:
          Bless you, Weewam. It only takes
          some thought.

                                        CUT TO:

EXT. EVRYDOC VILLAGE - NIGHT.

Angle: Sir Laurence's hand knocks on an old wooden door.

Seconds later, the door swings open. A peasant with a rag, tying up her hair, stands at the entrance.

                    LUDOVICA:
          May i help you, Sir?

                    SIR LAURENCE:
          After ten years, we shall see.

Ludovica stares at them.

                                        CUT TO:

INT. LUDOVICA'S "HOUSE" - NIGHT.

Lanterns gleam as the camera glides to a small wooden table, all gathered around it.

                    LUDOVICA:
          My father would not give it to
          you? Even when he knew what the
          Prophecy had stated?

                    EDRIC:
          We've come to know he is consumed
          by earthly desires. As you
          remember, the one whom the Key was
          originally given to, they would
          become what they possessed...

Ludovica listens.

                    SIR LAURENCE:
          Rowan Emphedor is wise, Lord
          Xerminine is corrupt, and King
          Lassell is occupied by the earthly
          and not the eternal.

Ludovica is teared up.

                    LUDOVICA:
          I see.

Wiping her eyes, Ludovica stands up.

                    LUDOVICA: (CONT'D)
          Yes, i will give you the key. May
          it not consume you.

                    SIR LAURENCE:
          Oh that is not our concern. It's--

The screams of The Stenes roar through Evrydoc.

                    LUDOVICA:
          The Stenes. They've--

                    EDRIC:
          The Key has been revealed, as it's
          glowing. They have come and will
          hunt us down!

                    SIR LAURENCE:
          We must retreat.

                    LUDOVICA:
          Please do.

Ludovica opens the front door for them, handing them the
key.

                    LUDOVICA: (CONT'D)
          Be safe, all of you.

                    BARTH:
          You, my lady, have been most kind.

Ludovica nods her head as they exit.

EXT. EVRYDOC ROYAL STABLES - NIGHT

The five board their horses and ride off, The Stenes howls
getting closer.

                    MEL:
          They're nearing us!

Suddenley a troop of Stenes glide towards them, ahead of
them.

                    SIR LAURENCE:
          To your right!

They turn abruptly to the right and the horses gallop
faster than ever.

                    EDRIC:
          We're almost to the gate!

Suddenley a Stene catches up and knocks Edric off his
horse. Edric yells in pain.

                    BARTH:
          Edric!

Barth rides past, grabbing Edric by the shoulder and
hoisting him alongside him. The horses ride, exiting the
gate as it closes on the Stenes.

                                        CUT TO:

EXT. OUTSIDE OF THE SOMBER FOREST - DAWN.

The horses slow down, on the brink of the Somber forest.
Barth and Sir Laurence help Edric off. In the background
Mel and Adi look petrified with fear. They lay Edric on the
ground. Blood is pouring from his broken arm.

                    SIR LAURENCE:
          He's been cut and broken--badly.

Adi unloads his satchel. He pulls a hankercheif out and
ties it around Edric's arm. Edric groans in pain. Blood has
stained the grass.

                    SIR LAURENCE: (CONT'D)
          He's lost lots of blood.

                    MEL:
          W-what's going to happen to him?

Sir Laurence looks back.

                    SIR LAURENCE:
          I don't know, Mel. I really don't.

                    BARTH:
          Mr. Edric? You alright?

Edric groans.

                    EDRIC:
          I don't--i don't think i can go
          any further, Barth...

                    BARTH:
          That's not true, Edric!

                    EDRIC:
          Go on without me...

                    BARTH:
          You are my friend, Edric. I'm not
          leaving you, i'm staying right
          here. Nothing will change my mind!

Barth looks back at the others. They nod. Sir Laurence
steps foward.

                    SIR LAURENCE:
          Barth's right, Edric. What men
          would we be to leave another
          behind?

Edric barely smiles.

                                        CUT TO:

EXT. ASHVALE PLAINS - BARELY DAWN.

Bluemist and Gwydion ride the horse across the open fields.
Stars twinkle their last as the sun rises in the east.
Bluemist smiles a smile of freedom. Gwydion stops the horse
to take a break.

                    BLUEMIST:
          It's wonderful.

                    GWYDION:
          It's just the norm, Ms.

                    BLUEMIST:
          No, it's freedom. I've been a
          slave,...to fear.

                    GWYDION:
          A slave you are, no more. Eh,
          where're we headed?

                    BLUEMIST:
          I'm sorry?

                    GWYDION:
          Where should we go?

                    BLUEMIST:
          I'd like to go home. Back to
          Summerlin.

Gwydion looks back at her.

                    GWYDION:
          We shall...

He clicks his mouth, and the horse rides to the sun.

                                        CUT TO:

EXT. EDGE OF SOMBER FOREST - MORNING

A small fire crackles and the silence of Ashvale is peaceful. Sir Laurence is the only one awake. He stares at the fire zoned out.

                    SIR LAURENCE:
          "Someones in grave danger. Someone
          you love, Laurence."

He comes into focus. Sir Laurence stands up.

                    SIR LAURENCE: (CONT'D)
          Someone i love!

                    ADI:
          Might you be well, Sir?

                    SIR LAURENCE:
          Someone i love, Adi. Who could i
          love that is not already dead?

                    ADI:
          Are you quoting her highness,
          Laurence?

                    SIR LAURENCE:
          Indeed. I feel it is my mother.
          She is in danger, we must go!

                    ADI:
          What about Edric?

                    EDRIC (V.O.):
          I'll be okay...

Adi and Sir Laurence turn around smiling.

                    ADI:
          Edric!

Behind them, Barth and Mel awake.

                    MEL:
          Aw, Adi, what's all the fuss?

                    ADI:
          Edric's going to be alright, Mel!

                    SIR LAURENCE:
          Glad to have you back, Edric.

Edric barely smiles, but glances at Barth. Barth grins and winks at him.

                    EDRIC:
Must we head into the Somber
Forest?

                    SIR LAURENCE:
We must.

                    MEL:
What's so wrong about that? Just
one more till Deeply.

Sir Laurence turns around towards Mel. The others watch.

                    SIR LAURENCE:
The Somber Forest is a dreadful
place. Within are your darkest
fears and memories, only yet to be
reborn. It's a place, we must
conquer.

The other three stare, listening well.

                    BARTH:
By what means? How is it so, Sir
Laurence?

                    SIR LAURENCE:
The ghosts of your past, and even
ghosts of others. Ghosts that will
repeat everything somber, right
before your very eyes.

                    MEL:
We must be brave. Edric's always
been brave. He's very wise,
indeed.

                    EDRIC:
I am not wise. Rowan has given me
wisdom, it's not my cause.

                    SIR LAURENCE:
With that, i say, saddle up...

                                        CUT TO:

EXT. THE SOMBER FOREST - DAY

The world seems to go dark. Wind blows their hair as they
ride their horses through the hollow path of the Somber
Forest. The sound of a death elf sings a frightful humming
tune. One by one each's face is shown, listening.

                    BARTH:
          I haven't seen or heard much yet,
          Sir--

Sir Laurence silences him.

                    SIR LAURENCE:
          The ghosts have come...

Sir Laurence looks to his right and sees a ghostly image of
his family being attacked by Stenes. He sees his father
struck in the head with a stone, he falls down dead. He
hears the sound of his mother shriek as a sword stabs her
side. Edric looks to his left and sees the ghost of his
past. The little boy Edric is sitting at the table, his
father and mother pouring all their attention on Finrod.
Barth looks to his left and sees the ghost of his worst
fear: Merida Bloom is prisoner, being taken to the gallows.
She is tied, and the man in charge pulls the rope. She
screams. The sight of that makes Barth sob as he rides,
following the others. Mel and Adi look to their right. Emma
Broomsteade and Daisy Greendale are dancing in the Warwick
square. Suddenley Stenes fly through, their black fog
covering the girls. Whey they clear up, Daisy and Emma ly
dead on the brick ground. Adi and Mel's eyes are flooded.
Sir Laurence lastly sees the figure of his sister be
dragged off by Stenes. Her screams echos in the forest.
Suddenly the great laughter of Lord Xerminine dominates
all.

                    SIR LAURENCE: (CONT'D)
          It's not my mother. It's my
          sister. Hah!

He clicks his horse and dashes off, the others following
quickly.

                    EDRIC:
          What is it?

                    SIR LAURENCE:
          Lord Xerminine has her!

                    MEL:
          Who?

                    SIR LAURENCE:
          My sister! They have Bluemist!
          Hah!

He clicks again and the horses run as fast as ever.

                                                  CUT:

INT. EVRYDOC CASTLE - DAY

King Lassell paces the castle. Suddenly the great doors
open and Ludovica is dragged in by a guard and thrown at
his feet. She immediatley hugs him, quite relieved.

                    LUDOVICA:
          Father!

                    MERLYLLSON:
          Ludovica, dear?

He looks up at the guard.

                    GUARD:
          Sir, the Key of Temporary
          Happiness!

                    MERLYLLSON:
          What about it?

                    GUARD:
          It's gone.

Merlyllson looks into Ludovica's eyes. He throws her back
onto the ground.

                    MERLYLLSON:
          How could you?

                    LUDOVICA:
          Oh, Father, they were kind men, i
          had to help!

                    MERLYLLSON:
          Betraying your own father?

                    LUDOVICA:
          Please, they told me you wouldn't
          help them! It was a prohecy!

                    MERLYLLSON:
          You have betrayed your father and
          your country, Ludovica!

Merlyllson looks up at guard.

                    MERLYLLSON: (CONT'D)
          Lock her up!

                    LUDOVICA:
          No, father, please--

He slaps her in the face. The room falls silent. Merlyllson
looks her in the eye.

                    MERLYLLSON:
          You are no longer a princess, you
          are now a stranger.

Ludovica cries silently as she is led away.

                    MERLYLLSON: (CONT'D)
          Jock!

A skinny, pale, servant comes to him.

                    MERLYLLSON: (CONT'D)
          Announce war with Ellison. And get
          me that Laurence and those
          Weewams!

                                        CUT TO:

EXT. DARK ASHVALE - DAY

The cold hair blows their hair as they ride out of the
Somber Forest. The gates of Deeply are on the horizon.

                    EDRIC:
          How are we supposed to get in?

                    SIR LAURENCE:
          Do you even know how important you
          are, Edric! You carry the Map of
          Deeply!

Edric looks down, the Key of Wisdom is glowing.

                    EDRIC:
          We're almost there. I feel it is
          swarming with Stenes.

                    SIR LAURENCE:
          The Map!

Edric pulls the map out. The south entrance glows.

                    EDRIC:
          The south entrance! It isn't
          guarded, we can get in there.

Sir Laurence and the others steer the horses south and head
on towards Deeply gates.

                                        CUT TO:

INT. DEEPLY CASTLE - DAY

VIEW: Lord Xerminine's boots stomp as he walks through the castle towards the dungeon. He opens the cell door so hard it breaks off it's hinges. He enters the cell and realizes it's empty. His mask turns to the open window.

                    XERMININE:
          Empty? It's time to kill!

Xerminine yells in anger as he stomps out.

                    XERMININE: (CONT'D)
          Corpz!

Corpz glides over to Lord Xerminine.

                    CORPZ:
          Yesss, my Lord?

                    XERMININE:
          She is gone!

                    CORPZ:
          I-i don't understand, my Lord. She
          was securley inside. I don't see
          how she could of--

                    XERMININE:
          Well she's gone. Tell me, how she
          could have escaped?!

                    CORPZ:
          I-

                    XERMININE:
          She was rescued.

                    CORPZ:
          I'm sorry?

                    XERMININE:
          You heard what i said, Corpz!

                    CORPZ:
          Who?

Suddenley, Lord Xerminine grabs Corpz's neck. Corpz gasps for air.

                    XERMININE:
          Find out!

Xerminine lets go and storms off, leaving Corpz gasping for air on the floor.

CUT:

EXT. DEEPLY WEST GATE - AFTERNOON

Sir Laurence, Edric, Barth, Mel, and Adi sneak around the
corner of the building. The door is gigantic, towering over
all of them. Edric opens the door slightly and glances
around. The inside is dark and still.

                    ADI:
          Is it clear?

                    EDRIC:
          Shh, yes...

INT. DEEPLY CASTLE - DAY

They all sneak in. Sir Laurence has his sword ready.

                    SIR LAURENCE:
          Be cautious. Any minute a Stene
          could appear and kill us all.

As they walk, Mel and Adi glance at each other nervously.
The four sneak down giant stone hallways. Suddenley a Stene
floats by and they dart behind a wall.

                    BARTH:
          (Whispers) Where would the Key be
          kept?

Sir Laurence walks ahead of them.

                    EDRIC:
          That's not his main priority,
          Barth. He's here for his sister.

The four Weewams follow Sir Laurence quicky and cautiously.
Sir Laurence looks left then right then heads straight. The
dungeon becomes visible and Sir Laurence runs to it. He
sees the door is off it's hinges. Sir Laurence looks around
in the cell and sees the blood on the floor and skeletons.
He kneels down and picks up Bluemist's old clothes.

FLASHBACK: Bluemist and Laurence and their parents are
eating at the Tavern.

                    BLUEMIST:
          Summerlin's a nice place. I've
          been wanting to visit for year,
          but i haven't ever had a chance
          because there's so much things to
          do back in Swanzy.
                    (MORE)

                    BLUEMIST: (CONT'D)
          Isn't the villagers nice here?
          Well, i think so.

Sir Laurence smiles at his father, Bluemist is talking a
lot.

                    SIR LAURENCE:
          I'm hearing you're quite excited?

Bluemist smiles.

                    BLUEMIST:
          Indeed.

Suddenly the scream of a Stene is heard. The door bursts
open and the Stenes come inside. The last thing heard is
Bluemist's scream.

                                        FLASHBACK END:

Sir Laurence's hands begin to shake. The others reach the
entrance.

                    SIR LAURENCE:
          She--

                    ADI:
          Where's Bluemist?

Sir Laurence fights tears hard. Suddenley he begins to
weep, holding her clothes to his face. Edric and the others
gather around, putting their hands on him.

                    BARTH:
          I'm sorry, Sir Laurence.

                    SIR LAURENCE:
          I was too late. I was too late.

He continues to weep.

                                        CUT TO:

EXT. EVRYDOC VILLAGE - DAY

A thousand plus soldiers on their horses gather in front of
the gate. Villagers watch worried and silent. King Lassell
is in the front on his horse. He clicks his mouth and the
horse rides, the others following.

                    MERLYLLSON:
          I have declared war with Ellison!
          We will fight for our rights!

A child clings to her mother.

                    MERLYLLSON: (CONT'D)
          All of us, will never worry about
          those foreigners again! I will
          protect you. Never you fear! Hah!

The horse rides off. The others follow. An old lady grabs
her son's hand weeping.

                    OLD LADY:
          Jamen!

                    JAMEN:
          Bye, Mum.

The old lady weeps.

                                                  CUT:

INT. THE DUNGEON - DAY

Sir Laurence leaves the clothes on the floor and gets up.
Suddenly a clash is heard, and Lord Xerminine.

                    XERMININE (V.O.):
          Jerk! How many times have i told
          you!

                    EDRIC:
          We have to run!

The four run out, fast. They run through halls and climb
stone steps. They get to the top and look out over the
plains.

                    BARTH:
          Oh, my...

The plains are completely covered with soldiers on horses.
In the front is Merlyllson Lassell.

                    MEL:
          It's King Lassell.

                    ADI:
          How did they know we'd be here?

                    EDRIC:
          Lassell knew we'd be looking for
          the Key of Corruptness...

                                                  ANGLE:

Merlyllson stares up and spots the five.

                    MERLYLLSON:
          There they are!

Horses draw near.

                    MERLYLLSON: (CONT'D)
          Men of Ellison! You have stolen a
          valuable possession of mine. If
          you return it unto me, we will not
          bother you. But if you refuse, we
          will kill you!

                                        ANGLE:

The five stare down.

                    MEL:
          Edric?

                    EDRIC:
          We cannot.

Sir Laurence steps forth.

                    SIR LAURENCE:
          We will not return it, for it was
          a gift. War we will have to
          endure.

                    BARTH:
          But, Edric, the Key of
          Corruptness?

Sir Laurence lowers his voice to them.

                    SIR LAURENCE:
          Adi, Mel, and myself will do our
          best to distract Lassell and his
          men. Edric and Barth,...it's up to
          you to find the key and end this
          once and for all.

                    BARTH:
          Yes, sir!

                    EDRIC:
          Come on, Barth!

The two Weewams dash out through another exit. Sir Laurence
holds up his sword and yells out.

                                        ANGLE:

Lassell's men roar.

                    MERLYLLSON:
          Kill them!

The men charge.

                                        CUT TO:

EXT. EVRYDOC DUNGEON - DAY

Ludovica hears the shouts and cries from the villagers
outside. She looks out the barred windows.

                    LUDOVICA:
          My!

Ludovica runs to the barred gate.

                    LUDOVICA: (CONT'D)
          Jesse! Jesse!

Suddenly a little servant boy runs up.

                    JESSE:
          Ludy?

                    LUDOVICA:
          Help me!

                    JESSE:
          But didn't your father--

                    LUDOVICA:
          I'm not asking you to break the
          rules, Jesse. I've known of the
          Summerlin massacre. Sir
          Laurence...his sister! Find her!

                    JESSE:
          But...where?

                    LUDOVICA:
          I'm guessing no further than
          Summerlin, although she could have
          fled. Nevertheless, go!

                    JESSE:
          No...

He begins to unlock the cell door.

                    LUDOVICA:
          Jesse--

                    JESSE:
          You come with me. I cannot leave
          you here.

She looks into his eyes and grins. They dash off.

                                                  CUT

EXT. DEEPLY CASTLE - DAY

Sir Laurence sharpens his sword on the stone of the side of
the castle. Adi and Mel peer at the men down below.

                    ADI:
          How can we win? Surely we are
          outnumbered!

                    SIR LAURENCE:
          Flee to the messengers outside of
          Deeply, not far. Tell them to send
          word to Warwick and Ellison. We
          need more men!

Mel and Adi nod and run away.

                                                  CUT TO:

EXT. DEEPLY GROUNDS - DAY

Two horses dash, carrying Adi and Mel as fast as they can
run. The two ride to the gate and meet the messengers.

                    ADI:
          Report to Christopher Streep of
          Warwick! Tell him to gather more
          Weewams and help us fight this!

                    MEL:
          And you! Send word to Finrod
          Grover. Tell him he must gather
          all the men in Ellison he can
          find! Quick!

                    MESSENGER:
          Yes, Sir!

The two messengers dash off on their horses. Adi and Mel
watch them carefully.

                                                  CUT TO:

INT. DEEPLY CASTLE - AFTERNOON

Edric and Barth run down a stone hall. Right as Barth is about to dash a corner, Edric pulls him back.

                    BARTH:
          Wha--

Edric covers his mouth tightly. An evil Stene sweeps past, not seeing them.

                    EDRIC:
          We can't keep at this. We must
          disguise.

                    BARTH:
          Are you insane, Edric? The only
          troopers here are Stenes, we can't
          do that!

                    EDRIC:
          Trust me Barth...it's all for the
          best.

Edric glances down at the key clutched in his palm.

                    BARTH:
          Where to?

                    EDRIC:
          Follow me...

Edric runs quickly down the stone hall. Barth follows. Edric looks to make sure they're clear then enters a room.

INT. DEEPLY CASTLE ROOM - AFTERNOON

It is dark and musty. Rotten potatoes are on the floor.

                    BARTH:
          What is this place, Edric? It
          smells horrible.

                    EDRIC:
          This is the Stene's eating
          chambers. Rotten potatoes are the
          only meal.

                    BARTH:
          Blimey.

Edric walks over to a pile of clothes in the corner. He sifts through them.

                    BARTH: (CONT'D)
          What's that?

Edric hands Barth a black cloak and helmet.

                    EDRIC:
          Wear it.

Barth puts on the helmet.

                    BARTH:
          Ugh...potatoes.

                    EDRIC:
          It'll have to do until we find the
          Key.

Suddenly the ghostly sound of a Stene flies past the open
door. Barth and Edric dart behind the door. They wait until
it passes.

                    EDRIC: (CONT'D)
          All clear?

Barth cautiously glances out.

                    BARTH:
          I think so.

                    EDRIC:
          Let's go...

They run out, all in disguise.

                                                       CUT

EXT. SUMMERLIN RUINS - SUNSET

Gwydion and Bluemist arrive at the dust, ashes, and dead
bodies of Summerlin. Bluemist hops off the horse. Tears
fill her eyes.

                    BLUEMIST:
          What happend here...

                    GWYDION:
          I'm sorry, Ms. I can't imagine how
          hard this is for you.

                    BLUEMIST:
          The last person i saw here
          was...Laurence, my brother.

She tries to smile.

                    BLUEMIST: (CONT'D)
          We were both excited to visit,
          since we'd just come from Swanzy.

Bluemist touches the face of a dead child. She starts to
cry.

                    GWYDION:
          We might as well find you a room,
          Ms. It's getting late.

He comes over to her.

                    GWYDION: (CONT'D)
          Come on...

                                                       CUT

EXT. DEEPLY GROUNDS - SUNSET

Sir Laurence rides his horse up to the tent of King
Lassell. The guards notice and stick their heads inside the
tent.

INT. THE TENT - SUNSET

                    GUARD:
          Sir, the Enemy is here.

                    MERLYLLSON:
          Let him proceed. I am not afraid
          of him.

The guard bows and exits the tent.

                                                    CUT TO:

EXT. DEEPLY GROUNDS - SUNSET

                    GUARD:
          The King will see you now.

                    SIR LAURENCE:
          Thank you.

Sir Laurence goes inside the tent.

INT. THE TENT - SUNSET

                    MERLYLLSON:
What must you say before i end
your life?

                    SIR LAURENCE:
I'd like you to make an agreement
with i and my men...

                    MERLYLLSON:
What men?

                    SIR LAURENCE:
We are expecting them tomorrow. It
is only fair that his highness
wait till morning to proceed war.

Merlyllson stands and shakes hands with Sir Laurence.

                    MERLYLLSON:
We will wait...but you will be
defeated.

Sir Laurence says nothing and exits the tent, leaving King
Lassell alone inside.

                                        CUT TO:

INT. STREEP'S HOME - NIGHT

Christopher Streep sits comfortably in his chair falling
asleep when a loud knock is heard at the door. He groans.

                    CHRISTOPHER:
          Who is it?

                    MESSENGER (V.O.):
It's a messenger.

                                        CUT TO:

EXT. STREEP'S HOME - NIGHT

Christopher opens the door and looks up.

                    CHRISTOPHER:
Where do you come from?

                    MESSENGER:
Deeply. A Weewam like yourself
sent me.

                    CHRISTOPHER:
Good Lord, what is it?

                    MESSENGER:
          He asks you gather troops to help
          them fight the war against
          Evrydoc, led by King Lassell...

Christopher thinks and mumbles.

                    CHRISTOPHER:
          Adi...Mel...Key...Edric!

Suddenly Christopher's energy pops to the surface.

                    CHRISTOPHER: (CONT'D)
          Yes! I will! Thank you, Sir.

                    MESSENGER:
          Yes, Sir.

Messenger leaves on the horse and rides off. Christopher
grabs his coat and runs down the village road.

                                        CUT TO:

EXT. WARWICK SQUARE - NIGHT

The Weewams dance and sing. Christopher runs on stage.

                    CHRISTOPHER:
          Stop! Stop, you!

They all stop and look at him.

                    CHRISTOPHER: (CONT'D)
          It has been a month since Edric,
          Barth, Adi, and Mel have left us.
          Well now they need our help!

The Weewams listen anxiously.

                    CHRISTOPHER: (CONT'D)
          King Lassell has declared war
          against them. And they need our
          help.

The Weewams cheer.

                    CHISTOPHER:
          Can we do that?

The Weewams cheer and shout "yes". Christopher smiles.

                    CHRISTOPHER:
          Gather your pitch forks, and
          gather you butter knives! Whatever
          it may take, we will help them win
          this cruel war! Who's with me!

All the Weewams cheer.

                                                    CUT

INT. DEEPLY CASTLE - NIGHT

Edric and Barth walk around openly, and the Stenes don't
seem to realize their true identity. Edric looks around.

                    EDRIC:
          I see the door. I know that's it!

The two look at a door different than the rest.

                    BARTH:
          That's the west wing, isn't it?

                    EDRIC:
          Yes, Barth. I don't believe--

Suddenly two Stenes grab them and drag them off.

                                                    CUT

INT. THE LEAPING LIZARD TAVERN, SUMMERLIN - NIGHT

Bluemist and Gwydion sit at a table alone. Gwydion drinks
his ale and Bluemist stares quietly at her bubbling drink.

                    GWYDION:
          Well, you have to drink something,
          Ms. You'll be parched.

Bluemist stares. Meanwhile Jesse opens the tavern door.
Ludovica follows.

                    JESSE:
          I'll bet we'll find someone here.

                    WAITER:
          No children in the tavern, lad!

                    JESSE:
          No, i'm not here for a drink, i--

Waiter turns to waiter's 1 and 2.

                    WAITER:
          Get them out of here.

Waiter 1 and 2 rush and try to push Ludovica and Jesse out.

                    JESSE:
          Wait! We just need to talk to
          someone.

Suddenly Ludovica yells out.

                    LUDOVICA:
          Sir Laurence is alive!

The tavern goes quiet. Bluemist sits up.

                    BLUEMIST:
          You lie!

Jesse and Ludovica push themselves from the waiters and
rush over to Bluemist and Gwydion.

                    JESSE:
          It's true. He came to see Ludy a
          few days ago.

                    BLUEMIST:
          I don't understand.

Bluemist's eyes are filled to the brim.

                    LUDOVICA:
          He went on a quest with Weewams,
          they were to find the third key,
          the Key of Corruptness.

                    JESSE:
          He's in Deeply!

                    BLUEMIST:
          Laurence?

Ludovica nods.

                    JESSE:
          We've come all the way here to
          find you.

                    BLUEMIST:
          Let me see my brother!

                    GWYDION:
          How do we know that these aren't
          filthy lies?

                    LUDOVICA:
          Because i saw the Key of Wisdom
          myself. It glowed like the moon at
          night. I gave your brother my
          father's Key of Temporary
          Happiness.

                    JESSE:
          What she says it true...

A tear rolls down Bluemist's face. She smiles.

                    BLUEMIST:
          Thank you. Please, take me to him.

                    JESSE:
          That is why we came.

Bluemist looks at Gwydion.

                    BLUEMIST:
          Gwydion?

Gwydion stares at them, examining each. He shrugs.

                    GWYDION:
          Let's go.

Gwydion and Bluemist follow Ludovica and Jesse out the
door.

                                                      CUT

INT. DEEPLY DUNGEON - MORNING

Edric wakes up to the mask and blue eyes of Lord Xerminine.

                    XERMININE:
          Trying to find the last
          key,...were you?

Edric stays silent and wakes Barth by shaking him. Barth
wakes and gasps.

                    BARTH:
          You vomit!

                    XERMININE:
          With do, please keep talking. The
          more anger fills my soul till it's
          enough to kill you.

Barth falls silent.

                    XERMININE: (CONT'D)
          Tell me...where have you hidden
          the other keys?

                    EDRIC:
          That doesn't concern you...

                    XERMININE:
          Oh, but they're not hidden. You
          have them with you. No need for me
          to take them.

                    BARTH:
          Isn't that what you want?

                    XERMININE:
          Oh, i can take whatever i want
          when i want it from whom i want
          it. The trick is one zap--poof!
          Dead.

                    EDRIC:
          We have a different power,
          Xerminine.

                    XERMININE:
          Oh, but you don't. Helpless
          Weewams, you are.

Barth stands.

                    BARTH:
          No, we are not.

Edric stands.

                    EDRIC:
          Love is what we have. Friends and
          faith we have, aswell. That, you
          have none of.

Xerminine stands and stares in their faces.

                    XERMININE:
          One zap and i could kill you now.

Edric steps to his face.

                    EDRIC:
          You were a child, weak and alone.

Lord Xerminine barely begins to feel weak.

                    EDRIC: (CONT'D)
          You were an orphan, left to die by
          your father Zion Lassell.

Barth looks at Edric confused. Lord Xerminine tries to hide
his feelings.

                    EDRIC: (CONT'D)
          You did not like your name, you
          didn't want to have any relation
          with the Lassell family so you
          changed names to Xerminine.

                    XERMININE:
          You know nothing.

                    BARTH:
          He does. And Edric's the friend
          you wish you had. But you don't
          because you have betrayed
          everything good, everything good!

                    EDRIC:
          You have. Your brother is out
          there about to take my men down,
          when really it's you who will be
          taken down. The war is on.

Xerminine falls to the ground groaning.

                    BARTH:
          Truth weakens one, more like
          humbles one to his knees.

                    EDRIC:
          Good day, Luca Lassell.

Xerminine is too weak to get up and Edric and Barth are
able to escape, leaving Xerminine to himself.

                                                       CUT

EXT. DEEPLY GROUNDS - MORNING

As the sun is fogged up by dark clouds as it rises. The
shadow of a thousand men march in the distance. Adi looks
out from the stone building and sees them.

                    ADI:
          Sir Laurence!

Adi runs and wakes Mel and Sir Laurence.

> ADI: (CONT'D)
> They've come!

Sir Laurence and Mel follows Adi to the end of the wall.

> SIR LAURENCE:
> It is true.

CUT TO:

EXT. DEEPLY GROUNDS - DAY

King Lassell sharpens his sword when the shouts of the men in the distance catch his attention. He looks.

> MERLYLLSON:
> Men!

A guard rushes to him.

> GUARD:
> Sir?

> MERLYLLSON:
> Wake the troops. War has come!

CUT

EXT. DEEPLY GATES - DAY

ANGLE:

Two horses race, side by side. Ludovica and Jesse on one, Gwydion and Bluemist on the other.

WIDE ON:

They steer the horses to a shaded tree, close but still far from the King's tents.

CLOSE ON:

> BLUEMIST:
> Where's my brother?

> LUDOVICA:
> Out there...

She points in the direction of thousands of men preparing to fight.

> BLUEMIST:
> He could die!

                    LUDOVICA:
We'll find him. But, if we want to
i have to stop my father.

                    JESSE:
Don't, Ludy! It's dangerous.

                    LUDOVICA:
I must defend the ones i love.
Jesse, stay with Bluemist. Gwydion
and i will be back soon.

                    JESSE:
Alright, Ms.

Gwydion follows after Ludovica.

                                        CUT TO:

INT. DEEPLY CASTLE - DAY

Edric and Barth are chased by angry Stenes. They run as
fast as they can go.

                    BARTH:
Why are they chasing us!

                    EDRIC:
We've weakened their king!

Edric and Barth reach the unique door and run inside.

INT. KEY ROOM - DAY

                    EDRIC:
Lock it!

Barth locks the door just as Stenes hit it. The window is
left wide open and the wind blows harshly. Edric grabs the
Key of Corruptness from it's stand on a table. Suddenly the
room almost blackens. Barth shrieks. Two glowing eyes stare
at them from the corner.

                    CORPZ:
Come to steal, haven't you?

                    EDRIC:
Go!

                    BARTH:
Wha--

Edric grabs him and they leap out the window. Barth yells as the fall.

CUT TO:

EXT. DEEPLY GROUNDS - DAY

Ellison, Warwick, Sir Laurence, Adi, and Mel charge after Evrydoc's men. They violently clash and fight with their weapons, killing others.

CUT TO:

EXT. CLIFF - DAY

Ludovica grabs a bow and arrows and goes to the edge of the cliff and shoots men below.

                    LUDOVICA:
          I feel the need to end this!

She shoots and kills a man of Evrydoc. Gwydion grabs large stones and throws them with great fury and power. It wipes out many Evrydoc men.

CUT TO:

EXT. DEEPLY GROUNDS - DAY

King Lassell severes a Weewam's arm and stabs a man of Ellison. Suddenly an Evrydoc man dies next to him by an arrow. King Lassell looks up and sees Ludovica shooting from the cliff. She doesn't see him. King Lassell's eyes fuel with fury.

                    MERLYLLSON:
          Ludovica...

He leaves the group quickly.

CUT TO:

EXT. DEEPLY GROUNDS - DAY

Jamen fights, hitting men with his shield but refusing to use the sword. He turns his head and sees King Lassell abandoning them. A man dies next to him. Jamen looks confused.

CUT TO:

EXT. DEEPLY CASTLE ROOF - DAY

Edric and Barth run along the rooftop jumping over high
areas and leaping long distances.

                                                    CUT TO:

EXT. CLIFF - DAY

Ludovica shoots another man. She doesn't see, but
Merlyllson is behind her.

                    MERLYLLSON:
          Traitor!

He pushes her off the cliff. She catches onto a rock but
screams. Gwydion stops throwing rocks and reaches for her
hand.

                    LUDOVICA:
          Father, please!

                    MERLYLLSON:
          Killing your own men, how could
          you!

                    LUDOVICA:
          Help, please!

                    GWYDION:
          Ludovica, dear. Grab my hand!

She reaches for his hand. He barely catches her. She
screams.

                    LUDOVICA:
          Don't let me go!

Merlyllson leans over the cliff, holding up his sword.

                    MERLYLLSON:
          You will now die!

As he's about to stab her and arrow shoots through his
head. He falls down on the ground. Gwydion looks back and
Jesse is standing there holding the bow.

                    GWYDION:
          Son! Help me--it's Ludovica!

Jesse runs down to the edge and reaches for her hand.

                                                    CUT TO:

EXT. SHADY TREE - DAY

Bluemist waits under the tree watching the battle.

                    BLUEMIST:
          No...no...this isn't right!

She looks down at an abandoned sword. Suddenly she grabs it
and runs after the battle.

                                             CUT TO:

EXT. THE CLIFF - DAY

Ludovica screams like never before. Her hand starts to
slip.

                    LUDOVICA:
          Don't let me die! Don't let me
          die!

                    JESSE:
          Please, reach!

                    GWYDION:
          I can't for much longer, i need
          help!

                    JESSE:
          I'm trying!

Suddenly her hand fully slips and Ludovica screams as she
falls to her death.

                    GWYDION:
          Ludovica!

                    JESSE:
          NO!

Gwydion screams and tears his shirt.

                                             CUT TO:

EXT. DEEPLY GROUNDS - DAY

Sir Laurence fights against a man and kills him. Suddenly
the harsh crash of Ludovica hits the ground, dead. Sir
Laurence stares. Jamen rushes over.

                    JAMEN:
          No!

He holds her bleeding head and looks above.

                    JAMEN: (CONT'D)
          Ludovica! She's dead!

He yells it as loud as possible. Some men stop fighting to
get a good look.

                    JAMEN: (CONT'D)
          King Lassell has abandoned us and
          murdered his own flesh and blood!
          The Princess is dead!

Some men tear their shirts and weep. By now many have
stopped fighting.

                    SIR LAURENCE:
          What shall we do? How can i help?

                    JAMEN:
          We need to surrender. STOP!

He yells out to them men.

                    JAMEN: (CONT'D)
          I announce! Evrydoc now fully
          surrenders to Ellison and will
          return home! The Princess is dead,
          we must leave.

Jamen reaches his hand out to shake Sir Laurence's.

                    SIR LAURENCE:
          We...we accept.

He looks down at Ludovica sadly.

                                             CUT

EXT. DEEPLY CASTLE ROOFTOPS - DAY

Edric and Barth are chased by Stenes who are nearly about
to trample them. They jump down into a hall and the Stenes
are about to kill them when suddenly all are shot with
arrows and fall down dead. Edric and Barth slowly turn
around. There standing is Finrod, Christopher, and the
other Weewams, their arrows lowered.

                    BARTH:
          My Lord...

                                          CUT TO:

EXT. DEEPLY GROUNDS - AFTERNOON.

The Evrydoc men begin to leave, carrying their dead ones with them. Gwydion is walking around when he sees Jesse crying at the stained blood from Ludovica on the grass.

                    GWYDION:
          Hey...

                    JESSE:
          If i had only reached, further--

                    GWYDION:
          You are a hero, Jesse. You killed
          evil before he destroyed so many
          other lives.

                    JESSE:
          How could i be,...if i could not
          save Ludy.

                    GWYDION:
          She is safe now. I know she is
          safe.

He lifts up Jesse's face. They stare into each other's eyes. From a distance Sir Laurence, Adi, and Mel watch.

                    ADI:
          Precious blood spilled, trying to
          save us.

                    BLUEMIST (V.O.):
          Laurence?

Men clear a path for Bluemist as Sir Laurence turns around.

                                        CUT TO:

INT. DEEPLY CASTLE - EVENING

A loud clank is heard as Lord Xerminine's boots step up to them. Edric, Barth, Finrod, Christopher, and the others watch.

                    XERMININE:
          You are trapped. I will end this.

Lord Xerminine zaps three Weewams dead right then and there.

                    FINROD:
          You have no power when you fight
          against many.

                    XERMININE:
          We'll see...

He holds out his hand to zap them again when Edric and
Barth step up.

                    EDRIC:
          It is finished!

Suddenley Barth and Edric put the three keys together and
the light wipes Lord Xerminine to the ground.

                                        ANGLE:

A crumbling mask is broken on the ground.

Lord Xerminine begins to slowly turn around.

                                        CUT TO:

EXT. DEEPLY GROUNDS - EVENING

Sir Laurence sees his sister. They stare at each other from
a distance both wanting to cry. Adi and Mel smile
excitedly. Bluemist steps up to him and sobs aloud.

                    BLUEMIST:
          I'm sorry, i left. I'm sorry Mum
          and Father died, if i hadn't--

                    SIR LAURENCE:
          Come.

He grabs her and they weep and hug at the same time.

                                        CUT TO:

INT. DEEPLY CASTLE - EVENING

Lord Xerminine slowly turns around. He is a man in his mid
50's and has dark hair and blue eyes. Edric takes a sword
from Finrod and points it at his thoat.

                    XERMININE:
          No...

Lord Xerminine begins to sob.

                    XERMININE: (CONT'D)
          No! Please, i beg you. Have mercy!

He cries hard, leaning his face to the ground. Edric holds
up the sword, ready to cut his head off. As he swings in
her stabs the sword into the stone.

                                                   CUT TO:

EXT. DEEPLY GROUNDS - EVENING

Bluemist smiles tearfully at Sir Laurence who grins back.

                    ADI:
          Pardon me, Sir Laurence...but,
          Edric...

                    SIR LAURENCE:
          Dear me!

                    BLUEMIST:
          What is it?

                    SIR LAURENCE:
          I will not leave you. Come with
          me.

Mel, Adi, Sir Laurence, Gwydion, and Bluemist run off
followed by other men.

                                                   CUT TO:

INT. DEEPLY CASTLE - EVENING

The shock of Edric not murdering Xerminine is unbelievable.

                    FINROD:
          No, Edric! He deserves death.

                    EDRIC:
          He does...but anyone deserves
          grace.

Suddenly, Mel, Sir Laurence, Adi, Gwydion, and Bluemist run
in. Edric glances back.

                    EDRIC: (CONT'D)
          Welcome, Bluemist...meet Luca
          Lassell.

Bluemist stares at her torturer tearfully.

                    EDRIC: (CONT'D)
          Dear friends, take Mr. Lassell to
          his cell.

Five other Weewams come and take Lord Xerminine away.

                    BARTH:
          That was a brave thing you did,
          Mr. Grover...

                    EDRIC:
          I couldn't have done it without
          you.

                    BARTH:
          They keys...

Edric looks down at the keys in his hand.

                                        CUT TO:

INT. THE WEST WING - NIGHT

Edric opens the west wing's door. Edric, Barth, Adi, Mel,
Sir Laurence, Gwydion, Bluemist, Finrod, and Christopher go
inside. Edric carefully places each key in it's slot. He
twists them in place and light fills the dark room. Edric
and the other squint as three doors open, filled with
light. Three elves, one white, one black, and one blue step
out from it.

                    ELIDA:
          Edric Grover, i see...Welcome to
          the end of the quest. Given the
          Key of Wisdom you become very wise
          indeed.

                    DORIAN:
          The Key of Corruptness turned the
          already selfish Luca Lassell to
          evil...for he possessed it.

                    MIST:
          The Key of Temporary Happiness
          turned the self loving Merlyllson
          Lassell into a prideful coward.
          Content did not proceed for
          long...as you have seen, his life
          turned to destruction in the
          end...

                    ELIDA:
          But you Edric, since then have
          become the Keeper of The Key,
          given by Rowan Emphedor. You have
          become very wise...that is your
          true destiny.

The bright light fades as the doors and all three elves
vanish. Edric and the others are left to ponder. Suddenly
Edric breaks down sobbing, falling to the floor. He is very
relieved.

                    EDRIC:
          I did it...i finished, it's
          over...

Barth kneels down, crying aswell.

                    BARTH:
          Yes, Mr. Grover. You've made us
          all very proud...

They all gather around, placing their hands on Edric.

                    EDRIC:
          We all did it...we all conquered
          the quest.

                                        FADE/CUT TO:

EXT. LEIDLECK LAGOON - DAY

Springtime has come and the sun is beautiful, and foreign
flowers grow. Weewams and men of Ellison are gathered.
Edric, Barth, Mel, Adi, Sir Laurence, Bluemist, Finrod, and
Gwydion are lined up in front of the crowd. Rowan stands on
the side. She walks up to the front.

                    ROWAN:
          Weewams and men of Ellison...we
          have gathered here today to
          recognize that without these brave
          men and women standing with us,
          and the many who have died, we
          would not be here today.

Some Weewams and menclap.

                    ROWAN: (CONT'D)
          They have shown great courage and
          strength and have conquered the
          quest of reuniting the three Keys.
          The result was Wisdom by a great
          amount of grace. I would like to
          award each a gift of honor...

Weewams and men watch. Rowan steps up to Sir Laurence. A
mer-man hands her a sword of rubies.

                    ROWAN: (CONT'D)
          A sword of rubies to Sir Laurence
          Rotan..."The Brave"...

Sir Laurence bows and recieves the gift. Rowan is handed
two golden buttons and steps up to Adi and Mel who wait
eagerly.

                    ROWAN: (CONT'D)
          Buttons of pure gold, given to
          Adelheid Ogden and Melville
          Diedrich..."The Faithful"...

Adi and Mel bow. Rowan is handed an emerald dagger. She
steps up to Barth who's eyes are filled with tears, he
tries to smile.

                    ROWAN: (CONT'D)
          An emerald dagger to Bartholomew
          Grader..."The Loyal"...

She hands him the gift and he bows. Rowan is handed a sling
of fine leather. She steps up to Gwydion.

                    ROWAN: (CONT'D)
          To Gwydion Brickenden of Orville,
          a sling of fine leather. May you
          be known as..."The Selfless"...

Gwydion bows and smiles. Rowan is handed a lovely blue
flower crown. She smiles as she steps up to Bluemist who
looks most beautiful.

                    ROWAN: (CONT'D)
          A flower crown, to Bluemist
          Rotan..."The Fearless"...

Bluemist smiles as Rowan sets it on her head, then she
bows. Rowan is handed a crystal bow and arrow and she steps
up to Finrod Grover.

                    ROWAN: (CONT'D)
          A bow and arrow made of pure
          crystal,...gifted to Finrod
          Grover..."The Clever"...

Finrod accepts the gift and bows. Rowan takes a deep breath
as she is handed a sword of topaz. Rowan steps up to Edric
Grover who is trying not to cry.

                    ROWAN: (CONT'D)
          To Edric Grover..."The wise"...i
          give him the sword of topaz.

He accepts it and bows. Weewams and men clap and cheer.
Emma Broomsteade blows Mel a kiss from the crowd. He goes
red. Finrod turns to Edric and whispers.

                    FINROD:
          Thanks for changing me...you're a
          wonderful brother.

Edric looks at him and grins.

                              FADE/CUT TO:

EXT. WARWICK SQUARE - NIGHT

Weewams laugh and dance for the happiness of the world is
back. Edric sits at a table and watches Barth dance with
Merida Bloom, Adi dancing with Daisy Greendale, and Mel
teaching Emma Broomsteade steps to a dance. Edric smiles.
Finrod and Lucee Lee sit down next to him.

                    FINROD:
          Don't mind if we join you?

                    EDRIC:
          Not at all.

He glances at Lucee in the eyes.

                    EDRIC: (CONT'D)
          ...I'm--i'm sorry for the way of
          my behavior a while back...

Lucee faintly grins.

                    LUCEE:
          It's not an issue, Mr. Grover.

It is shown that Lucee knows Finrod and Edric need to talk
after a while of silence.

                    LUCEE: (CONT'D)
          Well,...i'll just go get some
          punch.

She gets up and leaves. Finrod looks at Edric, eyes filled
with tears.

                    FINROD:
          You know...(breathes
          deep),...Father would be proud of
          you...who you've turned out to be.

Suddenly the Weewams grow silent. Edric and Finrod look
back as Christopher Streep comes to the front.

                    CHRISTOPHER:
          The reason for this gathering
          tonight is to celebrate the safe
          return of our fellow Weewams.

Christopher winks at Edric.

                    CHRISTOPHER: (CONT'D)
          But also to reconize that life is
          short, and the best way to spend
          it is together. So...i'd like us
          all, including the known Sir
          Laurence and Bluemist Rotan to
          join us in singing our
          anthem...Laurence?

Sir Laurence and Bluemist enter, taller than everyone else.
Bluemist sits on a seat and Sir Laurence comes onstage.

                    SIR LAURENCE:
          As a child i was always fond of
          singing. But my voice never had a
          purpose...until now...

The Weewams watch, moved.

                    SIR LAURENCE: (CONT'D)
          In the peaceful land of ours,
          within the bright green trees,
          there's a kind of love we know,
          that's larger than the bees, it's
          a kind of love that grows, in our
          very hearts right now, it's the
          love of a generation, raining from
          the clouds, (all sing) Warwick,
          Warwick, From the pond, to the
          bridge, to the seas, We hold to
          this very love, that's higher than
          the trees...

Zoom in on all the faces watching. From Bluemist, to Edric.

                                        FADE OUT:

                    CUT

          CREDITS

(CONT'D)